"WHAT ARE YOU DOING?"

"Seducing you," he admitted as he stroked the waistband of her pants.

"To what purpose?" she asked, her voice just above a whisper.

"Pleasure, angel. And perhaps a bit of intrigue to see if I can't evoke a reaction from you in the process."

Her blue eyes glinted with reproach. "That bears no practical reasoning whatsoever."

"Not everything is based on practicality, sweetheart." He slid his hand beneath her blouse to explore the bare skin beneath. "Some experiences are based on sensation."

He pressed his palm to her side and ventured higher, slowly. Goose bumps sprouted along the way, indicating she wasn't nearly as averse to his touch as she pretended to be.

"Stoicism is the result of avoiding emotion, but our bodies speak for us." He traced the underwire of her bra with his thumb and smiled when her cheeks flushed in response. "Do you feel warm, angel?"

"I—" She cleared her throat. Twice. "I fail to see the relevance of what you're doing."

Sethios trailed his fingers higher to find her pebbled nipple and rolled it through the fabric. "What if I offered you something useful?" he asked as he continued taunting her breast. "Would that put your mind at ease?"

She swallowed again as her gaze deepened to a midnight blue. He doubted she recognized the reaction, but he did. *Arousal.*

Mmm, it seemed Seraphim could indeed feel.

IMMORTAL CURSE SERIES

BLOOD LAWS

FORBIDDEN BONDS

BLOOD HEART

ELDER BONDS

BLOOD BONDS

ANGEL BONDS

BLOOD BONDS

LEXI C. FOSS

Editing by: Outthink Edits, LLC

Developmental Editing: Heart Full of Ink, Casey Harris-Parks

Cover Design: Covers by Julie

Cover Photography: JW Photography and Covers

Cover Models: Kristen Lazarus-Wood and Salvador Herrera

Series Logo: The Font Diva

Published by: Ninja Newt Publishing, LLC

Print Edition

ISBN: 978-1-950694-34-1

To Matt, for your constant understanding and support. You are my always. <3

BLOOD BONDS

BOOK FIVE

A NOTE FROM THE AUTHOR

Blood Bonds is a prequel of sorts to the Immortal Curse series. Sethios and Caro's story answers several of the burning questions raised in the first four books, which is why *Blood Bonds* is listed as book five of the series.

For the best experience, I would recommend starting at the beginning, but it's not required. If you are new to the Immortal Curse world, I've included a glossary with key terms and definitions. To the readers who have been with me from the beginning, you may notice a few new key terms as well. ;-)

All right, so, full disclosure: I wrote this story for myself because I craved a better understanding of key characters. However, I loved it so much that I decided to share it with my readers. I hope you enjoy reading it as much as I enjoyed writing it.

Cheers,
Lexi C. Foss

GLOSSARY

PRETERNATURAL BEINGS

Fledgling (noun): The child of a male Ichorian and a human female, who has not yet been reborn as a Hydraian; they do not typically possess supernatural or psychic gifts until their immortal rebirth.

Hydraian (noun): An immortal offspring of a male Ichorian and a human female, who possesses two supernatural or psychic gifts and does not require human blood to survive.

Ichorian (noun): An immortal being of unknown descent who possesses one supernatural or psychic gift and requires human blood to survive.

Immortal (noun): A general noun designating a being who does not age and is immune to natural human death.

Seraphim (noun): A being who belongs to the highest order of angelic hierarchy.

KEY TERMS

Arcadia: Notorious Ichorian club in New York City that also serves as the primary meeting location for the Ichorian government.

Blood Laws: A series of ordinances created by the Ichorian governing board in response to the Treaty of 1747.

Catastrophic Relief Foundation (CRF): A global humanitarian aid organization headquartered in New York City with a secret paramilitary unit designed to destroy rogue supernaturals.

Conclave: The Ichorian governing board.

Edict: A law or rule issued by the High Council of Seraph.

Elders: The original Hydraians who also serve as the Hydraian governing board.

Fated Line: Seraphim who can foresee the future.

High Council of Seraph: Seraphim governing board.

Nizari: Ancient Ichorian assassins who hunt and kill fledglings.

Nizari Poison: A green substance notorious for killing fledglings and preventing their rebirth.

Sentinel: A soldier in the CRF unit designed to slaughter rogue immortal beings.

Treaty of 1747: An armistice between Hydraians and Ichorians to cease fire and live in their designated areas. Those who opt to cross these boundaries do so at their own risk.

Part One
Immortal Bonds

"Seraphim do not indulge in pleasures of the flesh. It is a
human tradition that holds no value to eternal beings."

-Caro

Chapter One

Blood Edict

Disease.

Death.

Deceit.

Devastation.

Filth, humanity, and greed littered the nightclub as obnoxious beats repeated overhead. The humans would call it music. Caro called it hell.

Why would anyone enjoy this?

At least from her perch at the back of the room, it didn't rattle her teeth, unlike her experience on the dance floor. How those beings tolerated it, she had no idea. She preferred peace and quiet. *Tranquility.*

Not even ten minutes and she missed home already.

She would find Osiris, deliver the edict, and leave.

The poisoned one, as her kind called him, had lived among the humans too long and adopted his own level of greed. First, he created a bloodline of life-sucking abominations who referred to themselves as Ichorians, and then they went on to procreate with humans to create Hydraians.

Blasphemy.

She would slaughter them all if given the chance, but her superiors felt it was Osiris's responsibility to clean up his own mess.

Fine.

Caro crossed her jean-clad legs and tapped her foot impatiently.

Her notes stated Osiris owned this pitiful establishment, and the abundance of Ichorians slithering about confirmed it. They couldn't see or sense her as she sat in a cloud of invisibility—a trait that suited this mission. Except her quarry remained hidden, which defeated the entire purpose of being here.

The cushion beneath her shifted as someone sat far too close for her liking. She considered appearing just to tell him to fuzz off, but then he looked directly at her with bright green eyes.

"Not every day a Seraphim graces us with her regal presence," he murmured, his gaze assessing.

Something akin to shock swept over her. Or she suspected that was it. Emotions belonged to humans.

He stretched an arm along the back of the couch, grazing her shoulder in the process. "To what do we owe the honor, Your Highness?"

"How are you doing that?" she demanded after his fingers brushed her again.

"What are you doing here?" he countered.

"I don't believe that's any of your business."

"Oh, on that we disagree." He leaned into her personal space. "This is my territory, and you certainly don't belong here."

Well, that last bit was a reasonably intelligent deduction. As for the former… "How does one own a territory? Or are you referring to this dreadful place?"

His laugh vibrated their shared seat, and she found the sound oddly pleasant. Her kind did not revel in amusement often, if ever, but humans did. Except this being beside her did not possess a mortal soul, yet he didn't appear to be Ichorian or Hydraian either. Because he saw her and touched her.

She stopped misting since it only wasted energy in his presence. "What are you?" she asked while cataloging his features. Thick brown hair, olive skin, and over six feet tall with a muscular stature that indicated he led a healthy lifestyle. His symmetrical face and square jaw would be considered handsome by those who appreciated appearance. And he had dimples when he smiled, which he was not doing now.

"Tell me why you're here," he said, his voice underlined with power.

The rune on her lower back flared as she responded. "I have a message for Osiris." Her eyes widened. "How—"

"Tell me the message," he interjected with that same underlying authority.

Her mouth slammed shut, only to reopen as the words were dragged from her throat of their own accord.

"The High Council of Seraph hereby issues the following blood edict to Osiris: Your immoral activities of late are in direct violation with your purpose on this plane. Using your gift for the afterlife to poison the blood of humanity has earned you an additional five millennia of solitude. Leniency may be granted when, and only when, you rid Earth of your abominations. Failure to do so may yield further actions from the council."

Her hand flew up to cover her mouth, not that it mattered now. That was the entirety of the message, and she'd just delivered it to the wrong being.

"Interesting," he mused. "Well, you can't tell him that

unless you court death." He looked her over. "And I certainly hope that's not the case, gorgeous." He extended his hand. "I'm Sethios."

She stared at the masculine fingers as they wiggled tauntingly before her. The act of shaking hands was very human. She ignored his request.

"What are you?" Her demand sounded more like a mumble behind her palm, and probably looked ridiculous.

He grinned. "Tell me your name, and I'll answer."

A bizarre agreement, but one she wasn't averse to. She lowered her hand from her mouth to her lap as he dropped his own to his side. His opposite limb remained along the back of the couch where he continued to brush his fingertips against her shoulder. An odd gesture, to be sure, but not unpleasant.

"Caro," she said. "Now tell me what you are."

"Caro," he repeated. She rather liked the way it sounded from his lips. "I don't have a type classification, or at least not one that I've been told. What do you call the child of a Seraphim and a human?"

"An impossibility," she replied immediately. "Seraphim only breed with other Seraphim, and only when a progeny is required. Why would one breed with a lowly species?"

"For pleasure?" he suggested.

"Of what kind?"

He seemed to be gaping at her now. "The sexual kind."

"Why?"

"What do you mean, 'why?'" His tone held a note of incredulity that confused her. The answer should be obvious.

"Why would one engage in an act for sexual pleasure? It holds no intrinsic value, nor does it bear credence. Reproduction serves a solitary purpose, and a Seraphim would not choose to breed with a human. The progeny would be most unfruitful."

He laughed again, sending a tingle down her spine.

Oh, that really is a lovely sound.

"Well, then I suppose that's my breed. Unfruitful. Thanks for clearing that up, angel."

"Seraphim," she corrected. "And you're welcome, though I'm unclear as to what I've improved."

"Wow." He shook his head, still laughing. "You're proving all the rumors true."

She blinked. "Rumors?"

"About Seraphim," he explained. At her blank look, he added, "That you're all coldhearted, stoic beings with no thought or care for humanity."

Her brow creased. She didn't much like that definition of her kind. "I prefer intellectual, otherworldly beings with a practical view of the world."

"Sure, sweetheart. Whatever makes you feel better."

An odd phrase. "It is not about feelings."

"Because you're all unfeeling beings." He nodded. "Then the rumors are true."

Her frown deepened. He clearly required more information. "Your generalization is inaccurate. There are those of my kind who do, in fact, embrace emotion out of necessity." Only because their powers required it, of course. Most Seraphim with powers linked to humanity preferred life among the mortals as well. Caro, however, did not.

"And are you one of them?"

"No."

"Hmm. I see." He lifted his opposite hand and snapped his fingers.

A short Ichorian with spiky blonde hair sauntered over with a hopeful expression. "Yes, Sire?"

"Two bourbons, no ice."

She bowed. "Of course, Sire."

He refocused on Caro. "What am I going to do with you?" His green eyes danced over her fitted blouse and jeans, causing an uncomfortable sensation to stir over her skin. It reminded her of bathing in the sunlight for too long.

"I'm not sure I follow. What would you like to do?" Because she didn't intend to stay long, even though his mannerisms fascinated her. Like that thumb tracing her upper arm. Why did he do that? And more importantly, why didn't she stop him?

"Isn't that the question of the night," he murmured, his gaze darkening to a forest green. "Several ideas come to mind."

"Yes?" she prompted, waiting.

But as his mouth opened, the mood in the club shifted.

She didn't sense him so much as *know* Osiris was here. From the reverent gazes shifting throughout the room, she found his entrance point. A set of spiral stairs that led to a platform above. Of course. She hadn't thought to look there.

"Stay seated," Sethios demanded beside her. "Do not speak unless I tell you to, and do not mist."

She bristled at his tone and his commands. Her mouth opened to give him a piece of her mind, but no sound escaped.

What is this sorcery?

No matter. She would deliver her message and be done with all of this. Except she couldn't stand.

His words trickled through her thoughts as understanding dawned.

He'd compelled her again, just as he had when he forced her responses earlier.

How incredibly rude.

The blonde Ichorian started over with the drinks, but Sethios waved her off. Also rude. Not that she had wanted a drink, but his behavior required modification.

You will regret silencing me.

She displayed that thought with a glower that elicited a chuckle from him. "That look I'll allow."

Oh, when this spell wore off, she would kick his ass. Caro might not be the strongest Seraphim in existence, but her strength should outmatch his. Her bloodline of two immortals marked herself as superior to his tainted birthright.

"Sethios," a cultured voice murmured, drawing her companion's gaze upward to Osiris. "I thought you were leaving."

"I thought so too," Sethios replied.

Caro sighed in relief, happy to finally be in the presence of the one who could help her complete this distasteful mission. Except her mouth refused to cooperate again.

"What has you so distracted?" Osiris mused, his gaze trailing over Caro.

No sign of recognition.

Of course, that was the point. The council sent her because he wouldn't know her, thus making it easier to deliver her message. Osiris had a tendency of avoiding the Seraphim who visited Earth, but he couldn't avoid someone with an unknown identity.

Only one problem. She still wasn't able speak.

Well, hell. This wasn't going as expected at all.

Sethios drew his fingers up and down her arms, creating a flurry of gooseflesh in their wake. She shouldn't enjoy that nearly as much as she did, but something about the touch felt right. And she wanted him to do it again.

More sorcery?

"Pretty, isn't she?" Sethios murmured.

"Indeed," Osiris replied. "Where did you find her?"

"Wandering in places she doesn't belong." Sethios continued that stroking while he spoke, dividing her focus between his words and the bizarre heat he was stirring inside her. She thought it might be anger at his high-handed behavior. Or something else.

Osiris twined a strand of her light blonde hair around his finger and yanked sharply. Her lips parted with an *Ow* that didn't grace the air.

Because Sethios had silenced her.

Bastard.

Her stay on Earth would now extend to include killing him. Surely the council would approve.

Another tug brought tears to her eyes and a smile to

Osiris's face. "You've silenced her."

Sethios merely shrugged. "I may let her scream later, but I'm enjoying her obedience for now."

We'll see about that, she seethed.

Osiris brushed the hair-wrapped finger over her cheek and chin before letting her go. He smiled fondly at Sethios. "Well done, Son."

"Thank you, Father," her companion replied.

Caro's gaze widened with the exchange.

Father and son?

She knew about the Ichorians and the Hydraians, but nothing about the Seraphim procreating. But as she studied the pair, she saw the obvious likeness. Osiris possessed an ancient air that Sethios lacked, but otherwise, they resembled twins with their matching green eyes, olive skin, and dark brown eyebrows. They even looked the same mortal age of thirty or so, though Sethios's thick hair gave him a younger appeal than his bald father.

Oh, the council would be furious.

Sethios was a true abomination. Even worse than the offense of poisoning humanity with a tainted bloodline.

A Seraphim assassin would be sent here to destroy him.

Both beings studied her with amused expressions.

The horror they read from her features was likely misinterpreted to mean something entirely different. For she wasn't afraid of them but disgusted by the entire situation.

"Well, it appears you have an eventful evening ahead." Osiris winked at her before nodding to his son. "Enjoy."

"I intend to," Sethios murmured, hugging her closer to his sturdy chest.

She cringed, waiting for the repulsion to hit her, but something decidedly other graced her instead. Her heart fluttered, causing her breath to shorten.

An additional power? she wondered. *How curious.*

It worsened as he pressed his lips to her neck.

Did he feel her quickening pulse?

"Good night, Son," Osiris murmured.

"Night," Sethios replied from her throat. He scraped his teeth along her skin, sending more of those goose pebbles down her arms. She watched helplessly as her quarry sauntered off, hands in his pockets, with no idea as to why she had come in the first place.

The council would be displeased. Her mission was one of import and meant to be short, but the abomination beside her had ruined everything.

And why was he nibbling her neck like that? It tingled.

She squirmed, but he held her in place with the arm around her shoulder and a hand on her leg. The show of power stirred something deep inside. Not fear, because he didn't appear to mean her harm, but something wicked.

What is this plane doing to me?

"So Seraphim do react to pleasure after all," he whispered. "Fascinating."

He stood and held out his hand. "Walk with me. No fighting or talking, and no going ethereal on me."

She hated that her legs complied.

Whenever this spell wore off, he would be in a world of hurt.

Because she would kill him.

Slowly.

After she gagged him.

CHAPTER TWO

Entertaining a Seraphim

Caro's anger vibrated beneath the arm Sethios had thrown over her shoulders. He tried not to be amused by it but couldn't help the grin gracing his lips.

Her sapphire gaze reminded him of molten gems.

Oh, he couldn't wait to see what she did when he released her from his persuasive hold. He loved a fighter, and her lean form suggested strength and precision. A perfect candidate for the bedroom, minus the stoic bit. Though, her body reacted to his just fine. He suspected the lack of emotion may be related to inexperience rather than an actual Seraphim trait.

He guided them through the streets of New York City all the way to his building and up to his penthouse suite. One of the perks of living for millennia? Money. He knew how and where to invest, and his much older father's resources helped matters.

Not that he cared for the old man.

Actually, he rather hated him.

Nearly three thousand years beneath his shadow, watching endless murder and mayhem, exhausted and bored him. The only one who kept him sane was Ezekiel, and that said quite a bit about the situation considering his best friend's proclivities for assassinating fledglings.

"You can speak and move freely now, but no misting," he told Caro. "Fancy a drink?"

"I'm going to kill you." She said it so seriously that he laughed.

"Yeah? Then I'd better make this one hell of a final drink." He ignored her furious stare and sauntered into his oversized kitchen. *Wine ought to do.* He plucked a bottle of Mershano Reserve from the cabinet and poured two glasses. "Seraphim imbibe, yes?"

She responded by throwing a knife at his head. He caught it by the handle and set it on the counter. "I'll take that as a polite refusal, then." More for him.

He popped a hip against the counter as he sipped the red wine and surveyed her from head to toe. "Do most Seraphim dress to the times, or did you do this to fit in?"

Caro palmed another knife, suggesting he should have frisked her before letting her loose in his condo.

She didn't throw this one, though her eyes telegraphed her consideration of his position and the best way to hurt him.

Make your move, love.

Sethios relished an even match, and he suspected this one would provide a reasonable challenge. Though, she had to be younger than him since his father didn't recognize her. A good thing, as the old man had a penchant for drawing angel blood. Eviscerating such a beautiful woman would have been a waste of potential.

"Why do you keep looking at me like that?" she

demanded.

He enjoyed another sip of his wine, amused, then set it to the side and cocked a brow. "Like what, sweetheart?"

"Like I'm food."

"Maybe I want to eat you."

A frown tugged at her lips. "But you're not an Ichorian."

"That doesn't mean I don't enjoy biting." He did. Very much. And her visible shiver suggested she might enjoy it as well.

The level of intrigue between them shifted upward a notch. This woman provided a new opportunity—bedding a Seraphim who claimed not to feel. Evoking passion from her would be a delectable challenge, if entertaining. And seducing her into it would be vastly diverting.

She twirled the blade with skillful fingers. "How old are you?" she asked.

"A little over three thousand human years. And you?"

She blinked. "You've survived in secret for three millennia?"

He retrieved his wine while keeping a watchful eye on that knife in her hand. "Yes. My father felt it best for everyone to assume me to be an Ichorian, something I believe he did to protect his identity more than mine. Most of his progeny believe him to be a powerful being but have no idea it's his blood that caused their immortal rebirths."

Ezekiel knew the truth about Sethios and his father, but very few others did. It was a clever tactic to blend with the immortals rather than formally rule them. Sethios suspected that would change someday, but for now, his sire seemed content.

"But how?" she asked. "I understand why—the High Council of Seraph would have you assassinated immediately—but *how* has your existence remained hidden all these years?"

Interesting. He always assumed his birth was an abomination, but his father never confirmed it. Perhaps that was the true reason for keeping his existence a secret.

Though, that would imply his old man cared, and Sethios knew better than anyone that Osiris only looked out for himself.

"Surely someone saw you as a child, yes?" she pressed, her weapon stilling between her fingers.

"He told others at the time that he kidnapped me from my birth parents, which was partially true since he murdered my mortal mother when he no longer required her services." It happened such a long time ago that Sethios could say it without flinching, but the memory was forever burned into his heart. No seven-year-old should watch his mother die, especially in the horrific manner delivered by his father.

Caro nodded. "I've studied his cruelty."

"Have you?"

"Oh, yes. He's a legend among Seraphim—an example of what not to become."

Sethios snorted. "Sounds about right, then. He's a right ass here as well."

She paused, her blonde eyebrow inching upward. "You're not fond of your creator?"

"You tell me, angel. Is he the kind of being I should be proud to call 'father'?" He finished his wine and discarded the empty glass.

"Seraphim," she corrected, as she did before. "And no, not at all. He's creating an army on Earth while my kind are sitting by allowing it to happen without recourse, which is completely unacceptable." Her lips smacked closed and she covered them with a hand. "I have spoken out of turn. You forced me again."

He chuckled. "No, sweetheart. That was entirely you, and quite fascinating, if I may add, because I do believe you're right." He often analyzed his maker's motives, especially during the immortal war several centuries back. "He's cultivating great power. I daresay your kind would be in for a fight if you decided to pop down and stir up trouble."

She studied him. "You were able to compel me."

He grinned. "Yes."

"You shouldn't be able to do that."

"Why? Because you possess a rune to thwart lesser beings?" He prowled toward her. "As I've already explained, I'm not an Ichorian."

"You're not a Seraphim either," she replied, her tone haughty.

He backed her into the dining area wall and caught her knife-wielding hand as she tried to slice his cheek. She dropped the blade as he squeezed her fingers, thereby ending the battle before it started.

Pity. He wanted more of a fight. Perhaps he would provoke it out of her.

"I possess most of the Seraphim traits," he murmured as he crowded her. She attempted to punch him with her free hand, but he caught her wrist and pinned both of her hands in one of his against the wall above her head.

"I'm strong," he continued. "I can compel, just like my father, I can see through ethereal veils, and runes do not impair me."

"Can you mist?" she asked, her tone breathier than before. He took that as a sign to step even closer, creating a miniscule gap between their bodies. Every inhale brushed her perfect breasts against his chest, something they both seemed to notice.

"No, sadly, I was not gifted with that ability or with wings." The latter were only available to Seraphim in their ethereal state. That was how he noticed Caro in the club— her fiery blue feathers drew him in immediately. They practically glowed in the darkness. Had his father spotted her first, she would have suffered. He shuddered thinking of the pain and mutilation his father enjoyed dispensing to those he had no use for. Hence the purpose of Sethios's detour.

And maybe he'd been a little curious, too. A Seraphim in the Arcadia wasn't a typical sight.

"Why are you holding me in this manner?" she asked,

her head tilting upward to hold his gaze. "If you wish to secure me, surely rope would be easier."

He grinned. "Careful, angel, or I'll take that as an offer."

"An offer for what?"

Oh, this would be entertaining indeed. "Have you ever been kissed?"

Her brow furrowed. "Kissing holds no practical use and should be avoided, especially between humans. It enhances the spread of disease, and their lives are already so short."

"We're not human," he pointed out.

"Fair, but the act of a kiss possesses no relevance to a Seraphim. We only touch when sparring or procreating."

He parted her thighs with one of his own and grabbed her hip with his free hand to keep her from moving. "And have you procreated, angel?"

"Yes." An unabashed response. "I have one progeny in my line."

"And did you enjoy the process of fornicating?" He preferred the term *fucking*, but Caro seemed to favor formal terms.

She scrunched her nose. "Enjoyment is for humans."

"Is it?" He slid his leg upward, and her breathing quickened. "I find the act very pleasing."

She swallowed. "What are you doing?"

"Seducing you," he admitted as he stroked the waistband of her pants.

"To what purpose?" she asked, her voice just above a whisper.

"Pleasure, angel. And perhaps a bit of intrigue to see if I can't evoke a reaction from you in the process."

Her blue eyes glinted with reproach. "That bears no practical reasoning whatsoever."

"Not everything is based on practicality, sweetheart." He slid his hand beneath her blouse to explore the bare skin beneath. "Some experiences are based on sensation."

He pressed his palm to her side and ventured higher, slowly. Goose bumps sprouted along the way, indicating she wasn't nearly as averse to his touch as she pretended to be.

"Stoicism is the result of avoiding emotion, but our bodies speak for us." He traced the underwire of her bra with his thumb and smiled when her cheeks flushed in response. "Do you feel warm, angel?"

"I—" She cleared her throat. Twice. "I fail to see the relevance of what you're doing."

Sethios trailed his fingers higher to find her pebbled nipple and rolled it through the fabric. "What if I offered you something useful?" he asked as he continued taunting her breast. "Would that put your mind at ease?"

She swallowed again as her gaze deepened to a midnight blue. He doubted she recognized the reaction, but he did. *Arousal.*

Mmm, it seemed Seraphim could indeed feel.

He would be exploring that discovery to the fullest once she conceded.

"Wh-what could you possibly offer?" Her words lacked the punch she obviously meant to deliver. It pleased him immensely.

"I know Osiris's home location," he replied. "And I think you'll find there are very few of us with that information."

She trembled as he removed his hand to venture south. He wanted to test the limits of her desire.

"That's not useful," she argued, even as she arched subtly into him.

Oh, what he wouldn't give to be inside her head right now. The debate had to be amusing.

"No?" he asked as his fingers popped the button on her jeans and drew down the zipper. "How long do you plan to roam Earth, angel? Because Osiris doesn't frequent the Arcadia often. He only visited this evening for a Conclave, which I assume is why your council sent you tonight."

She fought to hold his gaze as he traced the seam of her panties. Silk. An interesting choice for a Seraphim.

"When is the next Conclave?" she asked on an exhale.

Such a sultry tone bemoaning sex. How could she not hear it?

Sethios explored lower, to the damp juncture between her thighs. "Oh, angel, you're not even providing a challenge."

He dropped his forehead to hers as he fought the urge to rip her pants off and fuck her against the wall. Because she was more than ready, and her kind didn't break. He could go as hard and as long as he wanted.

Damn.

The images bombarding his thoughts almost derailed his focus, but he reined them back.

There would be no slow introduction to sex, however, he would have her consent first.

And he might make her beg a little, purely for fun. After he fucked her at least once first.

"As to when," he continued, referring to her question regarding the Conclave, "it could be months or years. Unless you plan to cause problems in the city?"

Her throat bobbed as she tried to form words, but his thumb had found a spot she couldn't ignore. He played her skillfully, creating waves of quivers that started at her pelvis and rolled through every limb.

She tried to tug her arms free, but he held them steady, refusing to give her an inch. A power play, one he needed to win her over. She thought she was the higher being based on birthright, but he would prove her wrong.

His mortal mother strengthened him more than she knew. It's what grounded him and also granted him the power he claimed as his Ichorian gift. Hypnosis was very useful and close enough to compulsion that few realized the extent of his abilities.

Not that he wanted to use either talent on Caro now.

Fucking her into oblivion would be so much sweeter with proper consent.

"What do you say, angel?" he whispered, his lips brushing hers. "I'll give you the information you need in exchange for a night in my bed. Does that sound practical enough to you?"

CHAPTER THREE

Knives or Clothes

Caro shouldn't agree.

Surely Osiris visited the Arcadia more than Sethios implied.

Although, his comment regarding why the High Council sent her tonight was accurate. They had instructed her to wait until the Conclave finished, then approach her quarry.

But Sethios found her first.

And now he was touching her in enlightening ways.

She shivered beneath his devilish ministrations. The sensation he evoked baffled her. Both hot and cold, underlined in desperation. She didn't understand it but felt compelled to learn more.

Surely she could handle one night. And if she distracted him enough, he might give up the information early, thus allowing her to kill him. Her superiors would approve of his removal from this plane and would likely be thankful for her efforts.

He did something to her feminine parts that caused her stomach to tighten in the most delightful way.

What is this black magic?

Seraphim were not supposed to feel, but she certainly felt *that.*

During her one and only time coupling with a male, she merely lay there for the few minutes it took Adriel to finish his duty. There were no sounds or words, just an uncomfortable required mating to create a progeny. If only technology worked on Seraphim as it did on humans. Alas, fate worked her magic in mysterious ways.

"We cannot breed," she managed as he applied more pressure. It almost hurt but didn't. Her body shook from the foreign gratification.

"Not an issue, sweetheart," he murmured, his voice husky and low. "I'm sterile."

She nodded, understanding. "Fate would never allow your seed to prosper. It's an abomination."

He chuckled. "Careful, angel. You're making me want to teach that delinquent mouth of yours a lesson."

"Of what kind?" She already spoke several languages, including many of the ancient ones. What more could he possibly teach her? His age had nothing on her birthright. She prospered amongst the clouds, while he wandered on Earth.

He traced her lips with his tongue, shocking her into silence.

That... is rather pleasant.

It tingled.

Far better than a fist to the face, to be certain, but also wet.

He tastes like wine.

"Do we have a deal?" he asked against her mouth. "Or do you need more reasons?"

She swallowed. "How many minutes do you require?" He'd said one night originally, but she wanted a definitive timeline.

"Minutes?" he repeated, his amusement evident. "If I'm to give you what you need, then I require hours, love."

She blinked, startled. "Hours? Surely not."

"Agree and I'll show you why." He removed his hand from her jeans just as she was on the brink of something delightful. "I want your agreement, angel." He replaced the pressure between her legs with his thigh, and a warmth unlike anything she'd ever experienced shot through her bloodstream.

Unworldly.

That was the only word she had for it.

This plane is messing with my senses.

Still, a few hours of this bizarre experience in exchange for the information she needed and the potential opportunity to kill him did qualify as a practical use of time.

But she needed her weapons.

"Return my knives," she demanded as he explored the expanse of skin beneath her blouse again. He seemed to have an odd fixation with her breasts.

"Afterward," he said.

"Now," she countered.

His green eyes glowed with challenge. "And here I thought you weren't the kinky sort."

She frowned. "I do not follow your logic."

"You will," he replied. "But I want your consent."

"And I want my blades."

"You'll have them." He removed his touch from her abdomen and wrapped his hand around her neck. "But try to cut me and you'll regret it."

The threat underlining his words and position didn't faze her. She planned to stab him, not slice him.

"Fine."

He grinned as if seeing through her acquiescence. "So we have a deal, angel?"

"How many minutes, or rather, hours, do you require?"

"Seven ought to do."

Her eyebrows inched up. "Seven hours?"

"Yes. That equates to one evening."

Perhaps he intended to sleep as well? That would work well with her plans. She could learn a bit from his body, gather her intelligence, and then exterminate him while he rested. All practical reasons to agree.

Except… "What do you gain from this?"

"Satisfaction," he replied as he slid his hand to the nape of her neck. His fingers found a pressure point that resulted in a release of tension she hadn't realized was there.

Oh, I like that far too much.

He continued to massage the spot as his thigh moved subtly between her legs. So strange, and yet good.

"You provide a new explorative opportunity," he continued, his voice low. "Which is something I consider a rarity at my age."

"Because I'm a Seraphim."

"Yes." He trailed his nose across her cheekbone as he inhaled. "Your arousal is intoxicating, angel."

His lips went to her neck to press an open-mouthed kiss against her pulse. It left her shaking uncontrollably.

More.

Adrenaline seemed to mount inside her, but she didn't know how to release it. Everything felt so impactful and stimulating. Better than a fight, but more draining than a run. The perplexity floored her. She craved more of this exquisite confusion.

"All right," she whispered. "I agree to your terms of seven hours of my time in exchange for information on your father's location."

"Mmm." He nipped her throat before pushing back and retrieving her blades from the floor. She almost felt cold without him pressed up against her, yet his eyes kept her warm as they trailed over her skin.

Sethios held out her two weapons. "You'll wear these

and only these in my bed.”

She blinked. “Excuse me?”

Caro had worn a ceremonial robe with Adriel. He hadn’t even seen her thighs—just lifted the fabric, fulfilled his obligation, and left while she waited for the seed to root inside her. She’d done everything she could to ensure it would work the first time so she didn’t have to experience it again. Her due diligence benefited Adriel as well; male Seraphim weren’t keen on the emotional weakness associated with sexual climax.

“You wanted your toys returned and I’m granting them, but your clothes remain here.” He twirled the blades with a skill that indicated training. “Your choice, angel.”

She licked her lips. “I want my knives.”

“Then I want your clothes.”

She stared at him. “That’s—”

“Not practical,” he finished for her. “To you, perhaps, but I’ll show you just why it’s practical once you disrobe.” He continued shifting the dagger between his fingers with expert skill as he studied her. “I’m done debating. Either agree or don’t.”

“Fine,” she replied. “I accept your irrational request.” Nudity never bothered her. She kicked off her boots, yanked off her already unfastened jeans, removed her blouse and undergarments, and then held out her hand. “Knives.”

His lips twitched. “Eager to fight me, darling?”

No. He proved himself more than capable when he pinned her against the wall. A half-breed should not boast that kind of strength, but Osiris’s bloodline superseded her own. And apparently, his son inherited similar talents.

“I wish to finish our agreement so I may go on my way.”

“Do you now?” He flipped the sharp items in his hand and held the handles out to her. “My bedroom is down the hall. I’ll meet you there in five minutes.”

She eyed him curiously. “You do not wish to start now?”

“No, angel. Part of the fun is anticipation. You’ll see.”

She doubted that greatly but took her knives anyway. "Then I shall await you in the bedroom."

"Excellent."

Lying with a half-breed. That probably broke a rule somewhere, but he shouldn't exist to begin with, so she doubted one had ever been written.

She needed Osiris's location to deliver her message; therefore, this remained within the terms of her purpose. So what if a small part of her felt enlightened by the occasion to experience something new. It wasn't every day she mingled with mortality. This could very easily be chalked up to a learning opportunity. An in-depth exploration of the intimacies of the human world.

Yes.

All right.

Decided, she gave him a nod and started toward his room.

If anything, he would prove her theories right about drawn-out sexual intercourse being an unnecessary human act. Pleasure held meaningless principles. He would soon realize the uselessness of this arrangement, but at least she would have her information.

And maybe his life.

~*~

Perfection.

Curves, legs for days, long blonde hair, easily reddened skin… Oh, yes, Sethios would enjoy this very much.

But he wanted to teach Caro the art of anticipation first. The woman thought she had this all figured out, that she would remain unfeeling and passionless, but he saw the interest in her vibrant blue eyes. She didn't understand it and would definitely fight it, but he intended to win her over in the end.

Caro would bathe in pleasure, over and over again.

He sipped his fresh glass of wine and smiled. This was

one way to cap off an otherwise monotonous evening. The latest Conclave had resulted in two poor souls meeting his father's wrath in front of an audience.

Sethios once enjoyed the torture sessions, but lately, they lost their flair and allure. He understood the point was to strike fear in the hearts of the Ichorians and keep them in line, but the repetitious nature of it all had grown old over the centuries.

Something big was coming. He felt it in every fiber of his being but didn't know what. Perhaps Caro was the instigator, or just her message was.

It would be a shame to send her away in the morning. His father would undoubtedly torture and maim her before sending her back with his own message to the High Council. Just like he did the last time they sent someone to deliver an edict.

Why would they send such a beautiful creature here? They had to know she would suffer his wrath.

He set the crystal glass on the counter with a shrug.

Oh well. Not his business. He promised her a location and would give it, after he introduced her to pleasure beyond her wildest dreams. What she did from there didn't concern him.

He unbuttoned his dress shirt and tossed it onto the heap of clothes on the floor.

The way she undressed so effortlessly had entertained him immensely. A woman comfortable in the nude was rare these days, but Caro seemed perfectly at ease. Her confidence was underlined in ignorance, something he would enjoy fixing. By the time he finished with her, she wouldn't recognize herself.

Sethios added his shoes, socks, and undershirt to the pile but left on his trousers. He would make Caro remove them.

Right, then.

Time to have some fun with a naked Seraphim and her knives.

CHAPTER FOUR

Wings with a View

Caro admired the New York City skyline. She never understood the allure from above, but Sethios's floor-to-ceiling windows offered quite a view.

The city lights illuminated his room in brown and black colors, including the monstrous bed dominating a fourth of the space. Why he felt the need to possess such a large mattress was beyond her. He clearly valued sleep more than he did practicality.

She ran her thumb over the hilt of her weapon before twirling it in her hand, similar to the way he had moments ago. Stabbing him upon entry seemed like a valid plan. If she hurt him badly enough, he may be willing to give up the position of his father.

Or she could go through with his request for a night in

bed in exchange for information.

What sort of being considered that a practical request?

A humanized one.

The poor man had no idea how much this plane had devalued his spirit. Granted, his birth was an atrocity in its own right, suggesting fate had it out for him all along.

"Try, angel." His voice came from the doorway behind her. "I'll withhold my persuasive advantage to give you an even battleground, but we play for terms."

"Seraphim." She turned to meet his gaze. "And what game are you suggesting now?"

He stepped away from the shadowy entry and into the lights streaming through the glass. She already suspected he possessed an athletic form, but his lack of a shirt confirmed it. All lean, muscular lines, and an abdomen sculpted from hard work. She could admire that because she knew what that type of physique required.

"Well?" she prompted, waiting for him to get on with it.

His lips curled. "You're a warrior at heart, Caro. Show me what you can do with your toys."

She blinked. "You wish for me to fight you?"

"I desire you to try, yes."

Try, he had said. Twice. "You do not believe me to be capable of besting you."

"Not in the slightest, but I'm willing to handicap myself by not engaging my gifts. Unless you prefer me to put you on your knees now and start our seven-hour marathon?"

Such arrogance. "I'll never kneel for you," she said, meaning it. "And you should be cautious of who you underestimate."

His pupils flared with challenge. "Prove me wrong, angel."

"Seraphim," she corrected for the thousandth time. "Angels are a myth."

"Now you're stalling," he murmured as he prowled closer. "Show me something entertaining, or I'll fuck your mouth first. While you kneel."

Her blood heated at the threat of debasing her in such a way. "I did not agree to that."

"You agreed to a night in my bed, darling, which means you'll be playing by my rules." He moved into her personal space. "I'm running out of patience, Caro. You seemed—"

She sliced her blade across his cheek and ducked out of his reach before he could react. It put her back to the exit, giving her the advantage. "What happens when I win?"

He faced her. "When?" He tsked as he drew his thumb over the wound she had created. "When you lose, I'll fuck you until tomorrow." He started forward. "In whatever position I want, however I want, wherever I want."

She bounced on her heels, calculating his next move. "That doesn't answer my question."

"I prefer not to waste time on frivolities," he murmured as he shifted ever closer. "Try again."

His hands hung loose at his sides, giving him a false air of ease. Each step contained a lethal restraint and highlighted the predator lurking beneath the skin.

The man exuded danger.

Her pulse hummed with anticipation. Fighting was one of her favorite pastimes, though not many Seraphim enjoyed sparring. Most saw it as unnecessary, but Caro had sensed disaster on the horizon for decades now—a dark whisper in her ear. She hadn't bothered mentioning it to her High Council, for her young age and inexperience would be ignored.

That didn't stop her from preparing.

She flipped her knife and lashed out at his abdomen, but he jumped backward with a chuckle. "Better than expected, but not nearly good enough."

Her eyes narrowed at the insult. She hadn't been trying to hurt him before, but now she would.

He blocked her first attempt with his forearm, then countered her kick with his thigh. All testing moves on her part to gauge his reaction time, which she begrudgingly admitted to being quite good.

Caro threw one of her knives in an attempt to train Sethios's focus on catching the lethal item before it embedded in his skull.

She used his temporary distraction to mist behind him and slice his shoulder with her remaining blade. He spun mid-move, caught her wrist and whirled her in a circle to place her back against his chest.

"Not bad," he murmured, his lips at her ear. She drove her fist back toward his thigh, but he snagged her forearm and stopped the motion with the ease of a man much stronger than her. "Shall we play again, angel?"

Her chest heaved as she stole a necessary breath. He'd bested her far too quickly and without his use of compulsion. "You've been properly taught."

"For much longer than you've been alive," he said softly. "How old are you, Caro?"

No sense in lying to him. "Nearly a century now."

"So young." He nibbled her neck as he folded her arms across her stomach. "Your pulse tells me you enjoyed our little quarrel. Tell me, was it the thought of hurting me that excited you so? Or something else?"

"Fighting increases adrenaline, which is what you sense. Nothing more."

His chuckle vibrated her back. "Oh, Caro, you have no idea, do you?" He let go of her arms. "Drop the knife and place your palms against the window."

She released the weapon against her will. "That's not necessary," she growled as her hands touched the glass.

"As you lost, that's not your decision to make." He bent to retrieve the dagger. She had no idea what he did with the other but guessed he pocketed it.

"What now?" she groused, awaiting his next wave of compulsion.

"Quid pro quo, angel." He traced the sharp edge down her spine, hard enough for her to feel without drawing blood. "I bled for you, so you will bleed for me."

Her eyes widened. "Excuse me?"

"Shh." He used his opposite hand to gather her hair over one shoulder and kissed the back of her neck. "I'm still deciding where I wish to exact payment, darling. Don't spoil my fun."

The metal slid lower to her ass and then to the back of her thighs. Gooseflesh pebbled her arms as he dropped to his knees behind her.

"Wh-what are you doing?" She tried to face him, but her hands on the glass held her in place.

"Spread your legs for me," he said, forcing her to comply.

She jolted as the razor point met her inner thigh. "Sethios," she managed to say, her mouth going dry. There were far too many lethal options in that location.

"I've always been a fan of the femoral artery," he murmured. "And Seraphim heal so quickly."

Caro yelped as the steel pierced her skin in a quick, efficient move. She knew without looking that this gash was far deeper than the ones she inflicted on his cheek and his shoulder. Her Seraphim genetics would heal the laceration in minutes, but to maim her in this way seemed futile, if luxuriant.

"Beautiful." The word was a breath against her leg. "I consider us even, angel." His tongue soothed the ache as he laved the open wound he had created.

Confusion sifted through her thoughts.

Why is he—

Oh.

That's new.

Heat emanated from his touch, spreading upward to her center and beyond. She bit her lip to hold in the moan that threatened to escape her mouth.

It held no practical recourse to react or enjoy this.

He wanted a night, and she was determined to give him that with silence. Because nothing—

The pad of his thumb swiped through her sex so unexpectedly that her knees nearly buckled.

"Remain on your feet, palms against the glass," Sethios said. "No moving your body from that position until I give permission."

Her responding growl turned to a groan as his tongue followed the path of his thumb.

She'd never.

This wasn't.

"Wh—" She couldn't voice her thought. It shattered as his mouth closed around her clit. Caro knew the purpose, had seen it done a thousand times, read about it in a variety of reference guides, but never understood the real reason. Until now.

Her forehead hit the window as her limbs shook with the need to collapse. But his coercion kept her upright. It created an intoxicating mix of irritation, confusion, and bliss—all emotions she had no business experiencing.

But his tongue circled her in a way that overruled reason.

"I don't… This is…" Her breath faltered as waves of foreign warmth lavished her from head to toe. "A-acceptable."

If he responded, she didn't hear it over the beat of her heart. It reminded her of a drum, sounding rhythmically in her ears as she struggled to stand upright. Each flick of his tongue ricocheted violent shocks to her limbs.

Her nails clawed the glass in an attempt to fist her hands, but she couldn't obey that simple request. Sethios had forbidden her from moving, something her body remembered even while her brain faltered.

His thumb dipped into her sex as his opposite hand caressed her thigh. She had no idea where he put her knife, she would worry about it later.

Give in, a dark part of her begged. *Feel.*

No. Her logical voice was weak at best. *Don't give him the satisfaction.*

It's a learning experience. Embrace it.

Oh, Sethios.

Her knees trembled as the remaining vestiges of her

sanity shattered under his assault. Flames overwhelmed every inch of her, engulfing her in an inferno of lust. She recognized the signs, had researched them, but never thought to allow them.

Why have I lived without this? her spirit whispered. *Such a waste of life.*

His thumb left, replaced by two fingers as he thrust deep into her channel, hitting her in a place she didn't know existed. Her core clenched and unfurled as a climax took her over the precipice into sensation. She never expected it to feel... so... *hot.*

Intense.

Frozen in time.

Can't feel my legs.

Too much, oh it's just too much.

Caro shuddered, overwhelmed by it all and unable to process. And the sound escaping her mouth—she didn't know her lungs allowed that.

Somehow she remained standing through it all, just as he demanded, but it almost hurt to comply. Her legs begged to fold, her hands sweating from the effort, and her head swimming in a sea of forbidden emotion.

Sethios laved her deeply before leaving the apex between her thighs, his chuckle vibrating her deep within. "Oh, angel, you do not disappoint."

~*~

Sethios ran his palms over Caro's firm ass and up her shaking spine. The gorgeous blush tinting her pale skin pleased him immensely.

"You enjoyed that," he murmured as he placed a kiss against the back of her neck. "Now it's my turn." He threaded his fingers in her blonde hair and yanked her head back. "Drop to your knees and remove my pants."

No sense in wasting time. They had seven hours together, and he intended to use every minute. Once he took the edge off, they could begin properly.

Caro nearly fell under his command. Her nimble fingers found his belt as her drowsy gaze narrowed up at him. Oh, he approved of that look. It would be so much fun to fuck her mouth while she glowered up at him with that defiant gleam in her beautiful eyes.

"Careful, darling, you're giving me vivid ideas," he murmured as she slid down the zipper with far more force than necessary.

"Do they involve me stabbing you?" she asked, her tone holding a growl to it that he wished to replicate in bed.

"Now you're just teasing, Caro." His cock hardened with the memory of her trying to fight him, sans clothes. It'd been one of the most erotic experiences in his very long life.

They would play more with her weapons after he fucked her. He couldn't wait to test her limits. She'd barely flinched from him slicing her femoral artery—a wound that would have slowly killed a mortal. But she was already healed and very much alive.

She yanked his pants down unceremoniously, as if she didn't care at all that he'd gone commando beneath, but he caught the telltale flare of her nostrils. Her pupils dilated as well as she dropped her gaze to his package.

Not so immune to me after all, are you, darling?

Her orgasm had tasted so very sweet on his tongue.

The taste of victory.

He'd invited her to fight him knowing it would spike her adrenaline. Then he'd used pain to punch through her stoic walls, and it had worked beautifully in his favor.

Sethios palmed her face and smiled at her submissive pose. "I do so love a woman on her knees."

"If I could stand, I would," she replied, her irritation evident. So much heated emotion for a Seraphim. He loved it.

"You can stand," he murmured, offering her a hand.

She refused him, as he suspected she would, and lifted herself gracefully onto her feet. Her dignity and confidence floored him. So many women would be quivering by now, or lying on the floor in sobs, but she held his gaze with a furious one of her own. It only turned him on more.

"How would you like me to fuck you, darling? Against the glass or bent over the bed?" Why he offered the choice, he didn't know. Yet he waited with bated breath for her reply.

She eyed the window and his bed with interest, surprising him more. He expected a retort about the practicality of either position, but she seemed to be taking his offer seriously.

Fucking perfect.

Why couldn't his usual bed partners act in this manner? They all submitted to his will, while she stood beside him as an equal despite his obvious power over her.

"Window," she murmured as she turned to rest her palms against the glass again. "I like the view."

He smirked, amused. "Why do you think that's the position I want you in?"

She tilted her hips in a come-hither manner that surprised him. "You'll tell me if it's wrong."

"Too right," he agreed, dragging his thumb over his bottom lip. "Okay, angel." He'd give her a view she'd remember. "Mist for me, but don't leave."

She glanced over her shoulder as her wings appeared in a semitranslucent state, shadowing the room in gorgeous shades of light and dark blue. He explored the feathers with his fingertips and traced them to her spine.

"Can you extend them?" he asked, awed by their beauty. He definitely wanted to fuck her in this state.

Azure wings stretched before his vision as she did as he requested, shocking him. Seemed she was far more complicit in this game than she cared to admit.

"Keep them like that," he said, phrasing it as a demand but without the compulsion. She shrugged and returned to admiring the New York City skyline, but he caught the tremor in her spine. Whether she realized it or not, her body was not as indifferent to him as she wanted to believe.

He gripped her hips and lifted her without warning, leaving her feet dangling in the air.

She yelped in response, and her wings fluttered against his chest to hold herself steady.

"Hands on the glass," he reminded her when she struggled for balance. She clawed at the window as he positioned her right where he wanted and thrust into her from behind.

Her gasp told him he'd been too rough, but her warm, wet sheath squeezed his cock in eager welcome. He dropped his mouth to her neck and grinned as her feathers ruffled against him. "Too much, angel?"

"I'll adjust," she breathed.

"Yes, you will," he agreed as he rocked his hips slowly. Normally, he would fuck her the way he wanted, but her tightness confirmed her limited experience.

She required a languid introduction, and he desired her unfettered pleasure. Forcing orgasms out of her was part of what would make this so enjoyable.

She curled her calves upward to rest against the outside of his thighs. And damn if that wasn't her hottest response yet. It granted him deeper access as she balanced her upper body against the window and pressed her core against him.

The strength it took her to maintain that position, and the casual manner in which she did it, allured him to her that much more.

Hell, he nearly came from the act alone.

"Fuck, Caro." He pressed his head against the back of hers and reveled in her angelic being. New experiences were such a rarity in his too-long life that he wanted to extend the moment and enjoy it.

But his dick demanded attention.

"Feel free to scream," he murmured as he started to move in earnest. He dug his fingers into her hips as he slid home over and over again, taking his pleasure with a brutality that would destroy most humans. But rather than break, she shifted into him, meeting his thrusts and moaning each time he hit her G-spot.

Her body clearly had no problem giving into pleasure, and from the sounds spilling from her lips, he gathered she'd given up on fighting it. He grunted against her neck as he set a pace meant to relieve them both. Every groan from her lips felt like a plea to fuck her harder, leaving him no choice but to force her into oblivion with him.

"Come for me, Caro," Sethios demanded as he cascaded into an orgasmic state.

Her slick heat grasped him tightly, milking his seed as she shattered around him on a scream that sounded very much like his name. He grinned against her neck, loving every quiver and quake.

All night, he promised himself.

He would take her over and over and over again, until she couldn't walk.

And then he'd take her again.

Starting with the bed.

He didn't give her a moment to acclimate but pulled her away from the glass and tossed her onto the mattress. Her wings disappeared while her legs spread in undeniable invitation.

He would definitely bite her this time.

In several places.

"Again," he murmured as he crawled over her.

She blinked those gorgeous blue eyes up at him and nodded. "Yes."

Chapter Five

Game of Persuasion

Caro awoke in a daze, her head floating somewhere in the clouds. Her knives were long gone, as was her sense of reason.

Seraphim do not require pleasure.

Not true.

Not true at all.

Why did the council hide the truth? For male Seraphim to procreate, they had to ejaculate. Which meant they clearly had to feel *something* for an orgasm to occur. Yet, all this time, she had thought it was a physical reaction due to necessity.

Caro had never considered trying to excite herself because her superiors told her there was no point. The only Seraphim who embraced sensation and emotion were those who required it for their gifts to work, and Caro possessed no such need. Hence, she had never tried. And oh, how wrong she had been to deny herself this.

Sethios made me scream for him.

And I enjoyed it.

She quivered as the sensual memory of Sethios's body joining hers rolled through her thoughts. Her thighs clenched as a dark craving heated her blood. The muscular arm wrapped around her bare waist didn't help. If she rotated her hips, she'd hit his groin.

Would he understand the invitation? Would he accept?

Caro bit her lip to keep from groaning, both from need and frustration. This was the point where she should try to torture him for information and then kill him, not try to fornicate again.

Fuck, her mind corrected. That's what Sethios had called it. *Fucking.*

Seductive images assaulted her senses, causing her to squirm. She wanted more of those delicious feelings, the ones that left her limbs shaking and created stars behind her eyes.

It was so wrong but felt so right.

How many decades of her life had she spent in a cocoon of logic, refusing to experience emotion? Sethios had shattered her placative bubble and introduced her to a hidden part of herself. Would she ever be able to forget? To return to her previous self?

I've lost my mind, she realized.

It's this plane. It's messing with my sense of perception.

Or it's Sethios.

No.

Why would he alter her in this manner?

Perhaps to keep her from delivering her message to Osiris. Or as a way to protect himself from the inevitable. For Sethios needed to die. He was an abomination to Seraphim kind. Even if he did inspire explosions that sent her soul to a plane of nonexistence.

Ice trickled through her veins as her purpose slowly reappeared. If she failed in her mission to give the edict to Osiris, the High Council would send someone else, and Caro would be reprimanded.

She shivered at the picture of what that would entail. Seraphim couldn't be killed, but they could suffer. And that's what would happen if she didn't complete her task, especially if they learned about her evening in Sethios's bed.

Caro needed to remove herself from his grasp—now— or she risked losing more of her intelligence. Because this could not continue. To even consider extending their time together broke all manner of rationality. It was bad enough that she agreed to this exchange in the first place.

She attempted to dislodge herself from his hold and yelped as the world shifted abruptly. Her back hit the mattress as he pinned both of her wrists above her head in one of his hands.

"Good morning," he murmured as he settled on top of her. "Going somewhere?"

His intense green eyes smoldered, causing her pulse to jump. He'd given her that look last night right before biting her. She'd expected it to hurt, but instead it set her bloodstream on fire.

"I… Our…" She cleared her throat as she fought for control of her wayward mouth. "You owe me a location."

"Do I?" His free hand went to her hip. "And you were going to request that from me after rolling out of my bed?"

She licked her lips while considering how to reply to that. "I, uh, planned to get dressed first."

"Did you?" He arched a brow. "Interesting. Most women do not voluntarily leave my bed, nor do they do so without my express permission."

The man possessed an arrogance that ruffled her invisible feathers. "If you require me to request permission, then you will be waiting a very long time." She accepted his alpha tendencies last night out of pure enjoyment, but now they had her yearning for her knives.

Where did he put them?

He grinned. "Brilliant. I'm quite content to wait right here, angel." His hot arousal punctuated the point against her intimate flesh. "Shall I find a way for us to pass the time in the interim?"

Her thighs flexed as she fought the urge to arch into him. He would accept it as an invitation, one her body readily gave while her brain worked through escape plans.

"I upheld my part of our deal," she said while debating her next move. "You owe me a location."

He dropped his head to her neck and kissed the spot where he'd bitten her the night before. Her innate reaction to such a degrading act still floored her. She had enjoyed it far too much.

"Your pulse is singing, Caro." He breathed the words against her tender skin. "What has you so worked up, darling? The thought of another few hours in my bed, or the very real possibility that your mission will end badly?"

His tongue traced the column of her throat, eliciting a shudder from that dangerous part of her—the part that thought staying with him a few more days was the better plan.

"Or perhaps," he mused, "I caught you in the middle of a plan that involved your knives."

His grip tightened on her hip as he shifted and slid his thick erection into her waiting heat. She threw her head back on a growl-infused groan, both furious and enthralled.

Their night was done, and this act alone broke their deal, but her body refused to fight him. Her core had welcomed his penetration with a greedy squeeze that set her blood on fire. Again.

"Mmm." He pulled back slowly so the tip of him barely grazed her entrance. "I truly adore that sound, Caro. Make it again for me." He thrust into her so hard and fast that she had no choice but to comply.

"Sethios," she breathed, her fingers curling into fists. "This isn't—"

Another sharp flex of his pelvis silenced her protest.

Not fair.

He had three thousand years of experiencing pleasures of the flesh, whereas she only had last night. She stood no chance against his mastery.

"Were you saying something, darling?" he asked, his body resting over hers. "Do you wish to leave my bed?"

She shuddered. "I…" A violent tremor rocked her insides, sending sizzling energy through her limbs. Words failed her. Slicing him open with a blade seemed appropriate, but she also desired him to continue.

His virescent gaze grinned down at her as he studied her expression. "So much conflict," he murmured. "I still desire your mouth around my cock, Caro. Shall we do that now? Your indecision alone would bring me to the edge quickly enough. I won't know if you intend to bite or swallow."

"Biting," she moaned as he plunged into her again. "Definitely biting."

He chuckled. "Careful, darling. I might enjoy it."

Caro felt certain that he would, perhaps too much. He picked up the pace while holding her hips where he wanted them. It kept her from truly feeling the impact the way she desired, thus holding her on the brink of true enjoyment.

"Sethios." His name came out as a plea as she struggled to shift positions but couldn't.

"Need something?" he asked, his tone all lazy satisfaction as he slowed his movements.

"My knife," she grumbled, her hands clenching in frustration. Not that stabbing him would help, aside from providing some satisfaction.

"Mmm." He drew his nose across her cheek and released her hip. His lower body held hers with ease as she tried to take advantage of the freedom, and he tsked. "Impatience is not becoming."

"Taunting isn't either," she said through gritted teeth.

"No?" A sharp edge tickled her side, causing her breathing to falter.

My knife...

"Is this what you were looking for, angel?" he asked as he drew the weapon upward to her breast. He flattened the cold metal against her hard nipple. "I kept it safe for you throughout the night, just in case you thought up any intriguing ideas." He drove his cock into her so hard that she lost her train of thought.

"Sethios," she breathed.

"I love the way you say my name." He applied just enough pressure to the blade to pinch her skin without breaking the surface. "Say it again."

"Sethios." Her blood heated and cooled in response to his compulsion. The threat of his position was not lost on her, yet she couldn't will herself to mist away. She rather enjoyed the power play, even though it lacked logic. But not many men could control her in this manner, and he managed it so effortlessly.

"So pretty," he murmured, his manhood pulsing inside her.

She yelped as he nicked her tender nipple, drawing blood.

"Stop struggling, angel." He pulled out of her and dropped his mouth to her breast while still restraining her hands over her head. His tongue laved the wound as he created one right below it. Her limbs screamed at her to move, but she couldn't. He'd persuaded her not to struggle.

It should infuriate her, not send tingles of anticipation through her veins.

His hot mouth covered her taut peak, evoking a whimper from her. Electricity sizzled through the air as he pierced her skin with his teeth.

Abomination, her mind whispered.

More, her soul begged.

It created a conundrum she couldn't solve while her loins reacted to his touch.

She misted, then reappeared, and misted again as he tortured her with his mouth. He'd swapped breasts, and she hadn't even realized it. Her dagger rested in his hand at her throat, and she couldn't think enough to worry about it.

"Fuck, Caro," he whispered, his voice filled with awe. "I love that you don't break."

His words mingled with doubt in her mind because she felt broken. Seraphim weren't meant to enjoy pleasure, but Caro couldn't ignore Sethios's bite. It tingled and stung and left her shaking beneath him.

He released her from his hold and went to his knees beside her. A fire raged in his gaze as he took in her breasts.

"Turn over onto your stomach." Power underlined his tone. The feel of it titillated every nerve, urging her into the submissive pose by choice rather than by force. She balanced on her forearms and waited for his next command.

"Ass in the air," he demanded. Caro shifted onto her knees and jolted as the palm of his hand landed on one cheek. "You do not leave my bed without permission."

She glowered over her shoulder at him. "Try that again."

He grinned. "Happily."

His palm sliced against her backside once more, setting her blood on fire. She tried to move, to give him a piece of her mind, but her limbs remained locked while he watched in amusement.

"Unable to move, darling?" he asked, voice all innocence as he positioned himself behind her. "That's a shame, really."

"What have—"

He impaled her from behind, knocking the air from her lungs. Her forehead fell to her forearms as she fought to catch her breath under his harsh assault. Sensation mingled with pain as he took her body with a ferocity that would shatter most beings.

She fisted the blankets, her nails ready to rip the silk to threads. Each thrust rubbed the fresh marks on her ass, reminding her of his degrading act.

He *spanked* her.

The nerve.

If she had her blade, she'd stab him.

As if on cue, he pressed the sharp edge to her neck and nicked her skin. His tongue followed the sting as he draped himself over her back.

"Your fury is addicting," he murmured. "And provides the sweetest challenge."

She growled from beneath him. "I will kill you."

"Sure, angel." He kissed her neck. "Lift yourself onto your hands."

Her body complied even as her mind rebelled. Caro craved her sense of reason, anything to override the emotions boiling her blood—some convoluted mix of fury and arousal—because despite it all, her body loved everything he was doing to her and desired so much more.

This plane has destroyed me.

She shivered as he drew the metal down her rib cage and around to her breasts again. Rather than cut her as he did before, he gently brushed the tip against her hard nipple before trailing it downward.

"Stay very still," he murmured as the point touched her sensitive folds.

Lightning struck her insides, but his persuasion held her in place.

It felt too sharp, yet so good at the same time.

"Sethios," she breathed, her mind unable to think of more words to say. If she moved even an inch, he would slice her in her most delicate area, perhaps even himself since he remained inside her. But the dangerous edge rubbed her in just the right way, creating a hypnotic blend of terror and exhilaration.

This sort of act took trust, something she hadn't been ready to give him, but he'd left her with no choice.

And even while he exercised complete control over her, she felt the safety he offered. He wanted her pleasure because it increased his own. All of this was a way of testing her limits and forcing her to feel, and while she wanted to hate him for it, she couldn't. Not when he stirred such violent awareness inside her.

His lips caressed her shoulder as he continued his lethal ministrations below. He rocked into her carefully, deeply, stimulating a series of dark desires she never knew existed until him.

"More," she begged, her voice hoarse.

"Minx," he returned against her neck. His teeth pierced her skin—right at her pulse—shooting euphoria directly into her bloodstream. She had no idea Seraphim could do this, or perhaps it was only Osiris's line, but she'd never been more thankful.

Adrenaline mingled with lechery, sending her over the edge into oblivion. His name fell from her tongue on repeat as pangs of rapture fused with her soul.

I've forsaken everything.

But it was so worth the fall.

Her limbs held her upright by his sheer will alone because every part of her longed to collapse in a heap of bliss. But he took his pleasure from her, pounding into her welcoming heat, until he erupted on a groan that shook the room. The weapon disappeared as he rolled them to their sides, his mouth still against her neck and his arms circling her abdomen.

She fought to regain control, to think clearly, but nothing about what they'd just done allowed for reason.

Aftershocks hit her lower abdomen, sending shivers down to her toes, while Sethios calmly kissed her neck and whispered something foreign in her ears. She thought it might be Coptic, or another ancient language born before her time, but it was lyrical in sound.

"I don't understand," she whispered, her throat sore from screaming.

"I'm keeping you." He kissed her throat again. "For the time being, anyway."

She blinked. "What?"

"You heard me." He rotated her onto her back and gazed down at her with his alluring eyes. "I'm keeping you,

Caro." He kissed her cheek and rolled off the bed while she gaped after him.

"You can't *keep* me." A wave of dizziness hit her as she tried to sit up, forcing her to lie back down in his bed. *Okay, that was bizarre.*

"I can, actually." He opened a drawer while he spoke. "And I am, until we're done."

"That is not our agreement."

"Perhaps not," he said as he pulled on a pair of gym shorts. "We can renegotiate over lunch."

"I… This is not a negotiation."

"Not yet, no. But it will be. In the dining room." He smiled at her and opened his palm to reveal all her knives. *How? Where?* "Join me when you're able, angel. And don't even think of misting or disappearing on me. I have that well under my control."

He winked and sauntered off through the bedroom door while she struggled to determine how best to respond to any of that.

How did one fight such foolishness?

She couldn't stay here, not with her uncompleted mission. Nor did she *want* to remain with him.

Lie.

Right, well, her body wouldn't mind the extended holiday, but her brain required much more than a few seductive games to flourish.

She pushed off the bed and flinched at the onset of dizziness again.

What is happening to me?

Seraphim did not suffer from disease or bouts of weakness. But she felt positively awful.

Had he done something to her while she slept? Given her a command to respond to his acts in a human manner?

She frowned. Could he do that?

No.

This wasn't him so much as her—a reaction to the onslaught of foreign sentiments. Nearly a century living in stoic silence had numbed her and crafted an impenetrable armor around her angelic soul.

But Sethios had cracked it and forced her inner vixen to come out to play.

She expected regret to join her other emotions, except it didn't. Instead, she felt a strange surge of satisfaction and an equally strong desire to teach Sethios a lesson. Not out of anger or retribution, but out of pure challenge.

He'd commanded her as one would a child, spanked her as well, and then proclaimed to be keeping her. Well, she was not an object to be possessed.

It seemed he was in need of a lesson, one where she reminded him that Seraphim were the superior beings for a reason.

And for that, she required stealth, precision, and the perfect ploy.

Yes.

One last game before she left.

Then she would complete her mission.

CHAPTER SIX

Shattering Blood Bonds

Sethios smirked at Caro's clothes on the floor of the living area. Would she stalk out here naked for their negotiation? He certainly hoped so. And if she did so angrily, all the better.

A little nude sparring would suit his mood just fine. The knives were in his pocket, just in case she wanted to play again.

He grabbed two mugs from the cupboard and started the coffee maker. Surely Seraphim enjoyed caffeine. If not—

A familiar presence tickled his spine, interrupting his thought process.

Hmm. Bad timing. Normally, he'd welcome his best friend's visit, but Sethios preferred to taunt his angel without an audience. For today, anyway. Maybe he'd invite Ezekiel over to play tomorrow.

"E," he murmured as the Ichorian materialized beside him. "I'm in the middle—"

"He's coming." A hint of urgency underlined the words, causing Sethios to meet his friend's ebony gaze.

"Who?" he asked, curious.

"Your father."

Sethios snorted. "Right." Osiris never visited. All of their interactions were through summons only or during a Conclave. Sethios selected a third ceramic mug from the cupboard. "I assume you're staying for coffee."

Ezekiel snatched the mug and slammed it down on the counter. "Skye prophesied Osiris's demise, and it involves you and some unknown entity."

Sethios blinked at his oldest friend. "What?"

"He's already on his way here. We need to go. Now." Ezekiel reached for him just as Caro walked out wearing Sethios's clothes. "Fuck."

His best friend whipped out a knife and threw it without blinking an eye. The metal glinted in the early afternoon sunlight streaming through the windows as the sharp edge sailed toward Caro's head.

Sethios didn't think. He just reacted.

Mist to me. The command hit her faster than the blade, forcing her to shift to his side. Caro stumbled into him, and he caught her with his arm.

Ezekiel gaped at them, his eyebrows shooting upward. "Well, hello, unknown entity." Those gold-flecked eyes radiated awe. "A Seraphim?"

"Pretty, isn't she?" Amusement touched Sethios's chest as Caro growled at his diminutive tone. "And please don't kill her, E. I'm not done playing."

He mentally ordered her to remain still before she could react and smiled when she glowered at him.

"You can speak, darling," he taunted. *In fact, I encourage you to.*

Ezekiel shook his head as if waking from a spell. "We don't have time for this. You need to run. Now."

Sethios smirked. "Because of a prophecy." He'd been on the receiving end of his father's fury more than once and survived. This wouldn't be any different. Though, he might have to send Caro home first or force her to disappear. He wasn't ready to lose her yet.

"What prophecy?" Caro demanded. "And which seer delivered it?"

"Skye. She foresaw Osiris's death at the hand of his son and someone without a face."

"I'm not familiar with a 'Skye.'" She frowned.

"You wouldn't be," Ezekiel snapped. "I'm risking my life by being here, Sethios. Either come with me or face your fate, but I'm not waiting for Osiris to sense my presence here." He held out his hand and cocked a brow. "Decide."

Sethios considered and shrugged. "I appreciate the warning, E. But I'll handle it." He always did in one way or another. Besides, he also had a Seraphim at his disposal. She could mist them to anywhere in the world, or even to the angelic plane. A perfect escape mechanism.

Ezekiel shook his head, sadness radiating from him. "You always were a stubborn ass."

"Pot, meet kettle."

"Touché," his best friend murmured. "But do me a favor?"

"Sure." He'd try, anyway.

"Don't die on me. You're one of the few in existence I can tolerate." Ezekiel disappeared with those solemn words.

Sethios smiled. "Likewise, old friend. Likewise."

Energy drifted over him, the only indication that Ezekiel may have heard him, and then his friend's essence was gone.

"Hmm." Sethios poured himself a cup of freshly brewed coffee, followed by one for Caro. "Tell me what you have planned for Osiris." He threaded compulsion through the words, leaving her no choice but to obey.

"To deliver the message from the High Council of

Seraph."

"And what do you plan to do after that?"

"Kill you," she replied simply.

He grinned. "Well, now that isn't a threat to my father. He might be disappointed, but I hardly think he'd mistake it for his own demise." Sethios appraised her outfit choice of a white shirt and boxer shorts. "I approve, angel."

"Of my killing you?"

"Of you trying," he corrected. "Especially in my clothes."

"Mine weren't in the bedroom, and these were the only practical option."

"As I said, I approve." He was about to grant her permission to move when the hairs along his arms stood on end. "Well, then."

Sethios hadn't exactly doubted Ezekiel so much as wondered at the plausibility of his friend's claim. Osiris never visited the city without purpose, which indicated he'd taken this prophecy far too seriously.

This is going to be fun.

Or hurt.

Maybe both.

He popped his hip against the counter and picked up his coffee mug, the picture of nonchalance.

Caro stood beside him, hands fisted. "Free me." She clearly didn't feel the impending doom approaching them both.

"I don't think that would be wise," Sethios murmured. *In fact...* "Do not speak, mist, or move unless I give you permission." His tone left no room for flexibility or negotiation.

Fury radiated off her, something he would have found entertaining any other time.

"It's for your protection, angel." And his as well. "If I grab your hand and call you 'love,' then mist us to Paris."

He blew on his coffee before taking a sip. Poor Caro would have to wait to taste hers. He didn't trust her not to dump the piping hot liquid over his head.

Five.

Four.

Three.

Two.

Knock, knock.

Sethios set the mug down and sauntered into his condo's foyer.

"Father," he greeted as he opened the door. "This is a surprise." The latter was directed at the two Ichorian minions in the hallway. Their names escaped him. Not that it mattered. They were inconsequential anyway.

"Is it?" his father asked. His gaze searched the condo over Sethios's shoulder, almost as though he could feel Ezekiel's energy. He might. If he did, he would hopefully chalk it up to an old essence. Their close friendship wasn't a secret.

Sethios shrugged and moved into the kitchen to retrieve his coffee. It served as both a distraction and a way to be closer to his escape route, should he need her.

"To what do I owe the pleasure?" Sethios asked, his features schooled into a facade of indifference.

His father eyed Caro with interest, as did the two minions behind him. "Is this the woman from last night?"

"Yes."

"She's still alive." Not a question, but a statement shrouded in surprise.

Sethios lifted a shoulder. "She amuses me. For now." A truth that didn't require explanation. "I know how much you loathe this city. Why are you here?"

"Direct as always." His father's gaze hadn't left Caro. "Allow her to speak."

"You wish for her to scream?" Sethios grinned. "It is a beautiful sound, but I'd prefer to finish my coffee first."

"It wasn't a request."

No. It most definitely wasn't.

"Tell me why you're here," Sethios said instead, setting

the coffee down. "It's not for her."

"Do I require a reason to visit my only progeny?"

"Yes."

His father finally shifted his gaze away from Caro and nailed him with a look. "You're hiding something."

"Always." No point in denying that. "But that's not why you're here."

"No." His father stepped closer, his attention returning to Caro. "There is something familiar about you."

She didn't speak, move, or even blink.

Good, angel.

"Because you already met her," Sethios reminded, feigning boredom. "Stop showboating and tell me why you're here."

"Skye had a vision this morning—a disturbing one. But you already know that, don't you?" Ancient green eyes flashed his way. "I can sense Ezekiel's recent presence. We'll be discussing it later."

Sethios's brow furrowed. "Ezekiel's presence is a permanent fixture in my condo, Father. Unlike yours. Now, what vision did your precious toy foresee that has you acting all out of sorts?"

"Disarm," his father demanded instead. "Now."

So that's how we're going to play this.

"I see." Having no choice, Sethios set Caro's knives on the counter. "Those were to be used on her, in case you were wondering."

"Kneel" was the next command.

Right. There would be no debate or discussion, then— just a swift reaction to a potential future.

"Given your behavior, I'm guessing this prophecy paints me—your son—as some sort of threat." He spoke the words while falling to his knees under the persuasion. "And we are not going to discuss it formally."

They were statements, not questions, because his father's behavior already provided the answers.

Sethios had hoped to avoid this for at least a few more

centuries, but it seemed his father didn't feel the same. Perhaps he'd realized how powerful his son had become and sought any excuse to take him down.

Or maybe his father was just bored and wanted a new challenge.

Or the prophecy is self-fulfilling, and I will, in fact, be Osiris's eventual demise.

No matter the reason, it seemed Ezekiel was right to suggest that Sethios run.

There would be no reasoning with his father. He'd suspected as much but needed to see it for himself first.

Good thing he already had several backup plans for this scenario.

"It's disappointing that you trust a seer over your own flesh and blood," Sethios added, his tone flat. No point in conveying any emotion. It would neither help nor fix the issue at hand.

"Her visions are never wrong." His father sounded neither apologetic nor concerned. "We'll see how her prophecy changes once I've detained you. Indefinitely."

"That sounds ominous and impossible," Sethios murmured. *Primarily because I won't be complying with shit.*

"Come now. You've turned your conquest into a pet with a few commands. I'm more than capable of doing the same to you."

"I see." *It's come to that, then.* "And here I thought we might be able to discuss this civilly, but instead, you wish to make a puppet of me."

"It might be temporary."

Doubtful. "You've always wished to control me." Something he recognized millennia ago. "I'm surprised it took you this long to try."

"Who's to say I haven't succeeded already?" An evil grin twitched at the edges of his father's mouth, causing Sethios's stomach to churn. He recognized that look. It occurred at every Conclave, right before his maker indulged in his penchant for torture.

This fate was always inevitable.

Blood ties mattered little to most ancient beings. No remorse or sense of humanity existed in those past a certain age, except under unique circumstances.

For them, their father-son bond never truly existed. Sethios was an instrument to be used, not a son or a progeny.

There would be no mercy or leniency, especially if Osiris believed his next-in-line to be a threat. Which he clearly did, thanks to a seer's prediction.

It was a miracle that it took her this long to foresee such a future.

Because if anyone could overtake Osiris, it was his son.

But not today.

"Well, I suppose there's only one thing left to do," Sethios said as he reached out to take hold of Caro's hand. He shifted his gaze to hers. "Isn't that right, love?"

His compulsion triggered, tightening his gut as the world shifted around him.

Ezekiel's ability to trace was nothing like misting. Blasts of color nearly blinded him, the hues matching Caro's blue-and-white wings. Her arms found his neck as he wrapped his own around her waist, and they whirled through a foreign tunnel of light and sound that nearly rendered him unconscious.

And then they were standing in the middle of an alley in Paris with his back against a brick wall and a seething angel before him.

CHAPTER SEVEN

Bloodlines

"You bastard!" She slapped him across the face. Twice. "Now I have to mist back to your condo to talk to him, and he'll probably be gone already. At least I can grab my knives."

"Don't mist," Sethios managed before she could disappear. He put all his effort into that single command, forcing her to remain. It served them both to keep her alive right now.

She punched him, causing him to keel over into an uncharacteristic heap onto the ground. Fuck. That teleportation trick took a lot out of him.

He shook the ringing from his ears while reaffirming his persuasive grip. She fell to her knees beside him on a shriek as he forced her down to the ground and held her there.

He'd keep her like that until he could breathe properly again.

Threats graced his ears as she listed all the clever ways she intended to castrate him once she had her weapons again. His lips curled despite the discomfort radiating through him.

Note to self: I dislike misting.

Ezekiel's gift turned the world black, and in the blink of an eye, a new scene materialized.

Caro's transportation left him feeling sick and disorientated. Almost as if it'd been wrong to travel with her. No wonder his father rejected that part of his nature.

Sethios shook his head, forcing it to clear.

They needed to start moving. His maker would call on Ezekiel to track them. It was only a matter of time before his best friend located his whereabouts and reported them back to Osiris.

Sethios loved his ability to compel but hated how it could be used so effortlessly against him.

He forced himself upward, his legs shaking with the effort. They needed money, clothes, and transportation. Preferably in that order.

And he required Caro's participation, something she would not be giving willingly, if her continued threats were anything to go by.

Compelling her required energy, and he needed all of his strength if they were going to survive. He had no choice but to convince her to work with him or leave her behind.

"If you go to him…" Sethios paused to clear his throat. He sounded like hell turned over. "He'll destroy you."

"I'm not afraid of him."

Sethios seriously doubted her intelligence in that moment. "You should. I can control you, angel. Which means he definitely can, and unlike me, he won't just use it to fuck you."

She glowered up at him. "He can't hurt me."

"What makes you so sure of that?"

"I'm a messenger from the High Council of Seraph.

Harming me is an immediate death sentence."

Sethios grinned, though it lacked humor. "That won't scare Osiris. Ask your council what happened to the last one they sent here with an edict." His father didn't care about repercussions, and he certainly didn't fear the beings that cast him out.

She frowned. "I'm the first to be tasked with this mission."

He shook his head. "No, angel. You're not. The same warning was delivered over three centuries ago. You know what I think?" He didn't give her a chance to negate him. "I think Osiris harming you is precisely what your council is hoping to achieve so they have cause to intervene."

It seemed logical enough to him. Send a pretty little Seraphim down to deliver a message, then retaliate when she's tortured and maimed. Though, under that same theory, they should have reacted the first time around.

Her lips flattened while her eyes flashed with possibilities. "You're certain they sent someone three centuries ago?"

"Give or take." Sethios shrugged. "Time is irrelevant, but a messenger did arrive with a similar message that my father didn't appreciate. After spending an inordinate amount of time torturing the Seraphim who dared dictate to him, he filleted the man alive and presumably sent him back. Or he may have left the poor sod buried in a hole somewhere. I didn't stick around to find out."

The only way to disable a Seraphim was through burial, something his father taught him that day. He'd dug a hole in the earth and compelled the angelic being to enter it. His terror had been palpable even as he complied. It would have given Sethios nightmares had he not already been well acquainted with his maker's antics.

"Trust me, angel. You don't want to deliver that message."

"Why should I trust you?" she demanded, glancing pointedly at her still-kneeling position.

"You shouldn't." He released her from his compulsion, except for the misting. She immediately jumped to her feet and moved several paces away.

He ran his fingers through his hair and sighed. "Look, I won't force you to remain here. Staying alive matters more to me than worrying about your actions. But I promise you, conveying the decree to him won't end well for you."

He brushed his hand over his bare abdomen and glanced at the alley's street name for reference. As he didn't recognize the name, it meant he was nowhere near his condo. He'd have to compel her to mist him one final time unless he could convince her to work with him.

"Aren't you the least bit curious why we're wrapped up in a prophecy together?" he asked, thinking out loud. "I don't believe in coincidences, and as you're the only recent change in my life, this is all connected somehow."

"Tell me about your prophetess."

"Skye? She's one of my father's most prized possessions, and she's never wrong."

Her eyebrow inched upward. "Then you wish to terminate Osiris?"

"Destroy would be a more apt word." Sethios had no love for his maker.

"But he created you."

"And he also just threatened to turn me into a walking puppet," he pointed out. "I'm useful to him, but only when I'm obedient. And apparently, according to the seer, I'm no longer capable of compliance. Or, at the very least, I'm on the edge of betraying him. And if Ezekiel is to be believed, you are the reason for my pending betrayal. I'm dying to know why that is, angel. Any ideas?"

She slowly shook her head. "I've told you my purpose. I'm a mere messenger."

"Hmm." He drew his thumb over his bottom lip as memories of last night flashed behind his eyes. "I think you're far more than that. The question is, what?"

Caro frowned. "And you intend to determine this?"

"Yes." Among many other things. "But I won't be able to research anything if Osiris finds us here."

She licked her lips and straightened her spine. "He will be unable to track us."

"True, he'll use Ezekiel. He traces by blood, and he's tasted mine." At Sethios's father's command.

Caro gave him a secret smile, one that seemed almost sly. "Just as you've tasted mine."

An odd comment, especially when accompanied by that grin. "Not in the same way, but sure."

"No. That's not what I meant. My blood grants you temporary detection immunity."

He stared at her. "I'm going to need a better explanation."

"The council sent me because I can't be identified. It's why Osiris didn't recognize me as a Seraphim." She spoke as though her explanation should be obvious to him.

"But I identified you immediately."

She made an impatient noise. "You only knew because you *saw* me. My bloodline is the heart of aura concealment. I could be anyone, and while my essence runs through your system, no one can identify us."

Well, shit.

As if he needed another excuse to bite her. Caro taunted him enough with all that creamy skin on display and her angelic aura. To know that she could also supply him with infinite protection by a mere sampling of her blood proved her invaluable to him.

Now Sethios had no choice but to well and truly keep her. Because she provided him an escape he never thought possible.

Having her compliance would be a benefit, but he no longer considered it a requirement.

"How long does it last?" he asked.

"As you are the first to ever imbibe my blood, I have no idea."

Hmm, not the answer he wanted. "If I'm the first, then

how do you know your essence will keep me unidentifiable?"

She shrugged. "It's expected. Seraphim gifts thrive in the bloodlines, and while some are more powerful than others, they work relatively the same. Take yours, for example. Exchanging Osiris's bloodline with mortals grants them the gift of life, or, I suppose, resurrection. That's how he's been able to create an army of immortal abominations."

Disgust colored her tone, indicating a potential avenue for exploitation. She'd indicated her distaste several times, including her disapproval of Sethios's living status, but they could debate that later.

"You don't approve of my father's antics." Not a question.

She snorted. "Whether I approve or not matters little to my superiors."

"They have no intention of stopping him?" Because that went against his earlier theory about her real purpose here— to inspire a reason to intervene.

"If they intend to punish his actions, it will not occur soon." Her voice darkened just enough to confirm her feelings on the subject.

"And yet, the prophecy stated I would be his demise, with the help of an unknown entity. Presumably, *you*." He rose a brow. "Aren't you the least bit intrigued by that?"

She chewed her cheek, considering. "This prophecy— what were the words exactly?"

"Ezekiel didn't repeat it verbatim, but I intend to ask him at my earliest opportunity." Which would be tricky given Sethios's father's involvement. "What do you say to working together until we know more?" He'd be keeping her regardless of her answer, but he'd try this approach first.

Caro narrowed her eyes. "You want my blood so you can remain anonymous."

Lying to her earned him nothing. "Yes."

Her glower lessened slightly at his honesty. "And what do I get in return?"

"Potentially, the opportunity to destroy Osiris." Something she seemed to crave.

"Seraphim cannot die." So practical.

"True, but he can be incapacitated. As I mentioned earlier, I've seen it done to others of your kind." Another reminder that seeking out Sethios's father was not the brightest of ideas. "I say we learn more about the prophecy and go from there. In the interim, I will require more of your blood."

"And if I do not wish to give it?" she countered, an eyebrow raised.

He grinned, loving her defiance. "We both know that wasn't a request." He stepped closer, backing her into the wall. "Just as we both know you won't mind."

She glared up at him. "I do mind."

"Do you?" He grabbed her hips to hold her in place when she tried to move to the side. "Because your moans earlier suggested otherwise."

"That…" She trailed off as his lips brushed her throat.

His leg moved just in time to block her intended knee to his groin.

He chuckled darkly against her neck. "Tease."

She tried again to kick him. He lifted her off the ground and used his thighs to pin hers to the wall, then caught her hands before she could hit him.

"This foreplay is turning me on, angel." He placed her wrists against the hard surface on either side of her head and fully aligned his torso with hers. "I really hope you're right about your blood, because I'm about to waste a hell of a lot of time convincing you to work with me."

He circled her pulse with his tongue and smiled at her soft gasp.

Compelling her would be easier, but he fancied challenge over ease.

Besides, his time on Earth might be limited. Might as well enjoy himself a little.

He pressed an open-mouthed kiss below her ear before

nibbling her earlobe. "You're trembling, Caro." And it certainly wasn't in rage. "Tell me why."

Her hands fisted in his as her thighs flexed. Not the reaction of a woman trying to fight him, but one seeking friction. Whether she realized it or not, her body enjoyed his attentions.

"You want my blood and my compliance," she surmised, tone admirably flat. "What do I gain?"

"Opportunity," he replied softly. "You hate that your council hasn't stopped Osiris yet, and together, we might be able to take him down."

"What else?" she demanded.

"Experience." He drew his teeth along her sensitive skin, creating a wake of goose bumps down her neck. "Because I've awakened a craving inside of you that requires more." Not arrogance, but the truth. She could deny it all she wanted, but her body conceded his point, especially as she attempted to arch into him.

"You're… this…" She cleared her throat. "I still wish to kill you."

"That's part of what makes this so fun," he whispered darkly. "Lust mingled with potential threat is intoxicating." He nuzzled her pulse. "Work with me, Caro. Help me destroy Osiris. With your ability to mask our presence and my knowledge of his true power, we could be a formidable pair."

He'd considered removing his maker several times, but never to the point of plotting. Now that Skye had envisioned the possibility, however, he saw no reason to hold back.

Which begged the question—was the prophecy self-fulfilling?

Sethios had only been pushed to this point because his father showed up on his doorstep, prepared to harm. Had he not reacted at all, Sethios would have likely finished toying with Caro and sent her on her merry way.

Did Skye know she would set the ball in motion by

telling Osiris about her vision?

So many possibilities.

"Agree, angel." His lips skimmed her cheek to hover above her mouth. "Please."

The word tasted bitter in his mouth, but he desired her cooperation. If anything, to grant him full access to his abilities. Forcing an unwilling Seraphim to comply with his every wish would exhaust him.

And yeah, maybe a small part of him hoped she would agree. Just so they could have a little more fun together. It wasn't every day he found a woman who could survive his inclinations in bed.

"We need the precise words of the prophecy to decipher the true meaning." Her practical nature drowned in the breathless quality of her voice, causing him to grin. He'd already won. "Then we can decide our course."

"So you agree to help?" He phrased it as a question even though he already knew her response.

"For now." Her sapphire gaze held his. "And I will only agree to sharing blood to keep us hidden while we determine our next steps."

He grinned against her lips. "Okay, angel." *If you say so.*

He released her and stepped back.

She landed deftly on her feet, her hands falling to her sides. "I also want my knives back."

"Hmm, that might be an issue." *Because they're in the condo we can never return to.* "But I can procure new ones for you?" he offered.

Her lips pursed as she considered. "Will they be of similar quality?"

"Better quality," he promised, meaning it. He would never play with dull or lackluster toys. Only the best.

She nodded slowly, her blue eyes flashing. "All right."

"Excellent. Now I need you to transport us to the other side of the city." He gave her the address. "I have a place there that Osiris doesn't know about." He actually owned several around the globe. "We can shower, change, and eat.

Then work on our plan."

She held out her hand. "I accept."

"Excellent." Sethios thought she meant to shake on it, but when he pressed his palm to hers, the world morphed into a tunnel of blue feathers. Apparently, that was her version of confirming her compliance.

Except, the little grin she flashed him at the end said she'd done it on purpose. Her own form of payback.

So, that's how she wanted to play.

Okay.

"This is going to be fun, angel," he rasped, breathless from their short mist across Paris.

As soon as his head stopped spinning, he'd start a game of his own. One that would end with her begging him to fuck her. He'd start by giving her space, leave her in constant anticipation of him making a move. Then, when she lowered her guard, he'd tease her until she couldn't take any more, and only then would he give in to her craving.

And he'd enjoy every fucking minute of it.

Chapter Eight

What Now?

Caro slowly ate the sandwich Sethios had procured for her. It tasted fine—good, even—but she'd lost her appetite some time ago.

His words regarding her council's motives for assigning her this mission kept taunting her. The logic of his assessment could not be ignored.

If someone else had already attempted her task, why send her to repeat it?

Did they wish to provoke a cause for their intervention?

Torturing another Seraphim was strictly prohibited. Her kind considered it even more dire than sharing blood with humans. If her superiors desired a proper reason to annihilate Osiris, then using her as an instigator proved rational. She'd consider the same avenue, except for the part of subjecting herself to unspeakable pain.

Caro shivered as she took another bite.

Perhaps they had no idea of his treatment of the former Seraphim. She wasn't aware of one being tasked with a similar assignment, though she wouldn't be privy to the details. Only members of the council maintained that knowledge.

Sethios refilled their wine and eyed her speculatively. He'd been doing that for the last hour without saying a word. Fine by her. If he wanted to stare at her, then she would repay the favor. He'd yet to put on a shirt, even after taking a shower and changing into jeans. And while it served no realistic purpose, she didn't mind admiring his physique.

It was quite nice. Especially the way he used it when touching her.

Her lips twitched at the forbidden thought. Luxuriating in the pleasures of the flesh was so very human, and yet, it felt invigorating. The way he made her feel—alive—was unlike anything she'd ever experienced.

Which meant a tiny part of her had agreed to this madness because of the access to the luxury he provided. She enjoyed it, and he was right about her wanting more.

"Hmm," he murmured, eyes dancing over her. "Hold that thought. We need to strategize."

"What thought?" she asked, blinking innocently.

His lips twitched at the corners. "You can keep it to yourself for now, angel, but I know that look all too well. And yes, we'll be obliging it later."

He sipped his wine and set it on the side table before stretching his arms over his head. Muscles flexed and moved, drawing her gaze to his abdomen and lower. She wanted to taste him.

"We need to know what Skye prophesied," he said as he lowered his arms. "And unfortunately, any avenue I use to contact Ezekiel about it will be tracked by Osiris. He has an uncanny ability to persuade those around him without their realization, and he's no doubt interwoven several compulsion tricks into my best friend by now."

"Then we need something Osiris hasn't thought of," Caro replied. "Or rather, someone."

Sethios cocked a brow. "Do you have an idea in mind?"

"Yes." She'd considered it earlier when he mentioned the council's plans, and had already initiated her protocols. "My son."

Both his eyebrows shot upward into his hairline. "Your son?"

It seemed logical enough to her. "He's of my blood—thereby making him undetectable—and he's a warrior. This task will be simple for a being of his heritage." She also intended to ask his opinion on her superiors' motives. As Adriel's son, he might be privy to more details than Caro.

"A warrior, meaning what?"

She stared at him. "Adriel's line." Sethios's expression suggested he didn't understand. "Every Seraphim has a unique gift. I am a descendant of the concealment line. It's why I'm the perfect messenger; my aura isn't traceable. Adriel is the original of the warrior bloodline, similar to how your father is the Seraphim of Life and Resurrection. Are you not familiar with these family trees?"

He shook his head slowly. "In my three thousand years, Osiris never spoke of his heritage. I understood that he used his blood to create Ichorians, and in turn Hydraians, but he's never mentioned anything about family trees or his title."

"It's an old title, one he hasn't owned in several thousand years due to his exile. Part of his punishment was the inability to continue his line, which—seeing as you exist—clearly did not uphold. You might not be pure Seraphim, but your gifts are impressive."

Amusement flashed in his gaze. "Was that a compliment?"

She ignored him. "My son is the product of my bloodline of untraceables, otherwise known as messengers, and Adriel's warrior line. That is what makes him suitable to assist us. And I've already called out to him."

"You called out to him?" Sethios repeated.

"Yes, when we departed from the alley."

"Like telepathy?"

Osiris truly taught his son nothing. She'd be shocked if it wasn't so expected of the ancient immortal. Either he hadn't wanted to prepare Sethios for the future—likely—or he didn't respect tradition enough to pass on these key elements of Seraphim society.

"Those bound by blood can communicate mentally, but it's not telepathy. That's a different family of abilities. This is more of an emotion tied to instructions that is channeled through states of unconsciousness. He may hear me right away, or in a few days. It depends on when he decides to sleep." And knowing her son, it may be a while before that happens. "He'll find me when he hears my request."

Sethios's face drained of color. "Does that mean Osiris can do that to me? With compulsion?"

A logical jump in thought, however, not accurate.

"Osiris may send you a message of displeasure, but his persuasion does not extend to that state of being." She paused to sip her wine, needing some liquid to clear her dry throat. Caro almost pitied Sethios's obvious lack of understanding. These were key principles of their life. How he had survived three thousand years without them was beyond her.

"Blood bonds are a way to pass each other gifts, and they serve as unique family ties. Technically, you've tapped into mine by drinking my blood. If I were to imbibe yours, we would form our own bond of sorts that would allow us to telegraph to each other as well."

It would also grant her access to his gift just as she'd given him the ability to use hers, except the ties would be indefinite. She preferred to avoid that. Being bound to anyone for eternity did not appeal to her. That he was an abomination should be the biggest deterrent, but she found it to be a minor detail, for some reason. She'd examine that thought later.

"If I'm to follow what you're saying, then all of the mortals Osiris's blood has altered are technically part of my family line?"

"Essentially, yes, but it's not quite the same. You are the only one to receive the direct line of resurrection as Osiris's blood progeny, hence your ability to persuade and likely resurrect minions of your own. I imagine it's somewhat diluted due to your mortal mother, but Seraphim genetics would still command the majority of your essence. As for the humans imbibing the line of resurrection, they are merely gifted the opportunity of rebirth and immortality. Assuming they die within the allotted time period, of course."

"Which explains why some mortals do not transition into Ichorian status," he murmured. "Fascinating. I always wondered why that occasionally happened."

"Mortals are delicate beings. If the blood passes through them before death occurs, then resurrection can't be triggered. The essence needs to be active for it to happen."

"Yet, Hydraians can be turned at their choosing," Sethios replied, his tone holding a note of curiosity that she interpreted to be a question.

"The only reason Hydraians—as they like to be called— can choose their rebirth is because they are born into the bloodline. It's actually why they are stronger than their Ichorian fathers. They carry Seraphim blood in their system which is enhanced during their eventual resurrection, essentially meaning they are rebirthed twice—initially and again on mortal death. That's why they have multiple abilities."

She'd consider it all fascinating if it wasn't so incredibly wrong.

"You realize all Osiris's abominations need to be destroyed, yes?" she asked.

Sethios grinned. "Let's focus on my father, then we'll talk about the bloodline."

"Because you have no interest in eradicating them?" she

guessed.

"Considering I'm one of those 'abominations,' I'm probably not your best recruit. But I will help you with Osiris." He finished his sandwich and pushed his plate to the side. "Regarding your son, you said it might take a few days?"

"Yes, perhaps even a week. Gabriel does not sleep often."

"Gabriel," he repeated. "I don't suppose he'll be all that thrilled to meet me."

She grinned, amused at the thought. "No. He'll very likely try to kill you." And she'd enjoy the show.

"Then I look forward to meeting him." Sethios winked at her and stood with their plates in his hands. "In the interim, we'll remain here and see if you're right about your blood. Should Ezekiel appear, however, you'll need to mist us elsewhere immediately."

She wasn't worried but nodded her agreement. "Any particular place, or will it be of my choosing?" Because she'd love to drop Sethios off in the middle of the Pacific Ocean and watch him swim for a bit.

"Given the devious glint in your gaze, you will not be deciding. Take us to Billings, Montana. I have allies there that we will need." He gave her a specific address that she committed to memory.

"Noted," she murmured. *After you go for a swim.*

He disappeared into the kitchen and returned with two glasses of water. He set one in front of her but remained standing with his own. "What shall we do to pass the time, angel?"

She considered their options. There was so much he didn't know that she could teach him. She probably shouldn't, especially since she doubted he would live long enough to use the information, but it was the least she could do since his father had clearly failed him.

"Would you like to learn more about the Seraphim family lines and their unique skills?" she asked, thinking that was a decent starting place.

He appeared surprised as he dropped into his seat across from her. "I had another activity in mind, but I find your suggestion temporarily intrigues me more." He folded his fingers on the table and stared intently at her. "Please. Continue."

"Okay. We'll start with the High Council, as they are the eldest of the Seraphim lines, and go from there."

CHAPTER NINE

Protective Progeny

Caro stared at herself in the mirror. She appeared paler than normal. Even her hair had tinted on the white side. Very odd. She thought it might be related to her time on Earth, which had now reached nearly two weeks thanks to her son's lack of a response.

She'd sent him two additional notes of urgency with images of their location. Words didn't always convey through the bond unless spoken with intensity. It was a fickle science, one she truly needed to study more.

Her blue eyes appeared lighter, almost azure in color. She frowned and wandered into the living area, where Sethios sat in what she deemed to be his favorite chair. He appeared the picture of ease with his coffee in one hand, newspaper in the other.

And very human.

His green gaze lifted to hers. "Morning, angel."

"Is it?" She peered out the windows. Days were starting to escape her notice. They'd purposely not ventured outside for long periods due to Gabriel's expected arrival. She suspected Sethios hadn't tried to seduce her at all for the same reason.

Not that she cared.

He shouldn't be touching her.

Or that's what she kept telling herself, but her body felt almost antsy. As if she was waiting for him to make a move.

And when he didn't, disappointment nagged at her. It was a conundrum she did not need or want. Yet, it rode her spirit harder each time she laid eyes on him. He'd bite her once a day, and she found herself looking forward to those short moments. Almost as if she were an addict awaiting her next hit of euphoria.

She refused to react out loud, but internally, she moaned with unsuppressed relief each time his teeth met her skin. And she discovered, more than once, wanting to reciprocate.

I need to leave this plane, she thought, just as she had done every day since her arrival. She had considered going to Gabriel herself, but if the council caught wind of her presence, they would demand an update on her mission. An update she couldn't provide. Not until she knew more.

Not for the first time in her existence, she questioned their motives. She'd wondered initially why they didn't just send a horde of warriors down to destroy Osiris. Because of Sethios, she questioned the very purpose of her being here as well.

He seemed quite content to wait—an immortal with no sense of time passing. She could take a note out of his book of nonchalance.

Caro sat across from him and picked up the coffee mug waiting for her. Sethios always provided her with things before she asked for them, something that prickled her nerves. It was almost as if he cared—a preposterous notion. Neither of them had any business caring for the other.

She tasted the black liquid and promptly spit it back out, appalled. Sethios glanced up from his paper with a quirked eyebrow. "Not to your liking?"

"What did you do to this?" she demanded as she gagged on the taste left in her mouth.

He frowned. "Nothing. It's the same as yesterday's coffee."

She shook her head, disagreeing. "This is nothing like it was yesterday. It's bitter and repugnant." Her nose scrunched. "And it smells awful."

He set his paper and mug aside to grab her cup. After taking a few sips, he studied her with concern. "Caro, it tastes the same as it did yesterday. I didn't switch brands or styles."

Her stomach heaved in disagreement, and she took off for the kitchen to find some water to rid her mouth of the flavor. Sethios joined her, his brow crumpled. She drank straight from the faucet and found it didn't help.

"I feel…" She trailed off and grabbed the counter to steady herself. "I don't feel right."

Sethios caught her hips as her legs gave out, and he lifted her into his arms. "You're very pale, Caro."

"I noticed," she said, dizzy. The ceiling seemed to spin as he carried her into the living area.

"Have I taken too much blood?" he asked.

She tried to shake her head, causing the room to whirl around her as a result. Her stomach churned with discomfort, something that rarely happened to Seraphim, if ever. "I… no." It wasn't blood loss. But the sensation reminded her—

"She's pregnant," a familiar voice announced. Energy stirred as Gabriel appeared before them, his expression bored and his arms folded. He eyed her the way he always did—without feeling. "Hello, Mother."

Caro sighed, relieved. "Gabriel."

Sethios's arms turned brittle beneath her.

"Pregnant?" he asked, voice low and radiating an emotion she couldn't define. "Caro is pregnant?"

Her brow furrowed. She'd been so distracted by Gabriel finally arriving that she hadn't really *heard* his announcement. "That's…" *Impossible* clung to her throat, refusing to grace the air.

Because that's exactly how she felt.

Weak.

Tender.

Light-headed.

Pale.

Those were all symptoms she experienced during her pregnancy with Gabriel. But how had he known that?

"Explain." The word came out far raspier than she intended.

"As I assume you already know how it happened, then you're likely asking me to explain how I know." Gabriel leaned against the wall, crossing one ankle over the other. "It was entirely impractical for the council to send you on this mission when my skills make me the better candidate. So I investigated—which is what took me so long to respond to your summons—and I learned that the fated line suggested you for this assignment."

"Fated line?" Sethios repeated.

"Seers," Caro whispered, resting her head against his shoulder. He had remained standing, his arms firm around her as he held her effortlessly in the air. She'd have found it strange at any other time, but her body currently appreciated the comfort.

"The ones you mentioned who all have the ability of foresight like Skye?"

She started to nod, but the motion did little for her equilibrium. "Yes."

"And they foresaw Caro's pregnancy?" He directed that question at her son.

"Yes. With your child." Gabriel pushed off the wall and

stalked toward them. "I thought it had to be wrong, that there was no way my mother would fall pregnant by an abomination, but apparently, she did."

He almost sounded disgusted, something that ruffled her feathers. But she didn't have the energy to defend her actions. Another spasm rocked her, forcing her to bury her head in Sethios's shoulder to keep from crying out.

This was just like her first pregnancy—the sudden sickness that hit her out of nowhere.

Damn. If things continued as they had the first time, then she'd be out of commission for, well, she didn't know.

Sethios's genetics weren't standard. Human gestational periods were nine months long, while Seraphim were closer to two.

"Oh God…" She cradled her stomach.

Caro had an unknown essence inside of her.

An abomination by Seraphim standards.

Her heart sped up at the thought.

They would kill her, or at the very least, the being growing inside of her.

Gabriel could be here now to carry out the order…

Horror unlike any she'd ever felt riddled her spirit, causing her to shudder.

No.

Procreation only mattered when the fetus was viable.

No.

To carry a child to term that would not be full-blooded Seraphim provided no practical use.

No!

Why go through the pain of pregnancy for an unfit being?

NO!

"Caro!" Sethios's shout bled into her thoughts, forcing her to focus on his face. Anxiety mingled with fury in his features, his green eyes storming with unfettered emotion.

"Calm. Down." The demand slapped her across the face, forcing her body into submission as she relaxed against him.

Only then did she feel the warm moisture running down her cheeks.

Tears.

She'd been crying?

Impossible.

Seraphim didn't feel enough to cry.

What is wrong with me?

There's a foreign life growing inside of me.

Her future child. An anathema. Someone who will be hunted to the edges of the earth for extermination.

She touched her abdomen.

My blood.

My progeny.

My duty to protect.

"That's an impressive gift," Gabriel said, voice flat. "Is that how you convinced my mother to fornicate with you?"

Sethios snorted. "Hardly. I may use it as a benefit in the bedroom, but I do not fuck unwilling women. And trust me, your mother was *very* willing."

The growl that pierced the air caused her heart to falter. Gabriel's icy green eyes were narrowed, the only indication that the sound had emanated from him.

"Refrain from speaking of my mother in such a way, or there will be consequences. She deserves respect and reverence, not crude language from a foulmouthed monstrosity."

"Gabriel," she breathed, shocked at the lethal undercurrent in his words.

His gaze met hers unapologetically. "You're surprised that I would defend you? I would not exist without you, Mother. I am inclined to feel at least somewhat protective about that."

Just as I feel innately protective of the life growing inside me.

She blinked.

Did this defensive need qualify as an emotion? Or an animalistic instinct?

"Two Seraphim who exude emotion. Does that weaken

or strengthen your position?" Sethios asked, his tone casual despite the intensity vibrating through the air. He clearly did not perceive Caro's son as a threat, which she deemed a mistake. Gabriel might be younger, but he possessed power unlike many other of her kind.

Her son blinked at Sethios, his expression morphing into stoicism. "When you're done using my mother as a shield, we can have that conversation."

"Posturing. I approve." Sethios dropped his gaze to Caro. "Your color is returning. Do you want to try standing, or would you like to continue being my *shield*?"

She frowned. "You can't fight Gabriel."

"No?" He arched a brow. "Then how am I to react when he attacks me?"

She laid her head against his shoulder again and focused on her son. "You can't fight Sethios."

Gabriel shrugged. "That remains to be seen, but I promise not to kill him."

Her stomach cramped, causing her to wince. Of course her body chose today to succumb to weakness, during the moment she most needed to be strong.

"What did the seers say about my purpose?" she asked, returning the conversation back to something pertinent.

"You were never meant to complete your assignment. Sethios was your target all along." His green gaze lifted to the man holding her. "Your child represents a future possibility the seers wish to see fulfilled."

"The unknown entity," Sethios whispered, his expression morphing into one of awe and skepticism. "But how is that possible? I've fucked numerous women over my lifetime—so many that I've lost count. None of them have ever fallen pregnant."

"Caro is a full-blooded Seraphim, and it seems your genetics were a perfect match for breeding."

Sethios didn't appear convinced, which she didn't know how to interpret. It wasn't like she fornicated with another man recently, or even within the last three decades. He had to know his seed was the cause.

"Fine, but my mother was a mortal. The human influence is why Hydraians can't reproduce, or that's always been my understanding, anyway."

"Perhaps." Gabriel shrugged. "I imagine your father's genes overrode much of your mother's, which is the reason you were able to procreate with Caro. Further, according to the seers, you are ideal mates for one another."

"Meaning they anticipated this and wanted it to happen," Caro added, uncertain of how to feel about that.

"Yes." Gabriel folded his arms. "I'm guessing the council didn't inform you because they didn't want to tempt fate."

"They don't know you're here," she realized.

"No. I discovered all of this on my own after learning of your assignment. Your summons only expedited my research. What appears to be the issue?" His gaze dropped to her still-flat stomach. "Aside from the obvious, I mean."

"Osiris's seer prophesied his pending demise at the hands of his son," Caro replied. "We wanted your help in learning more about what she foresaw, which you've already discovered."

Sethios's thumb traced a pattern against her hip as he held her seemingly closer. "I'd still like to know exactly what Skye told my father, as well as his plans for tracking me down."

"Interesting," Gabriel said, his hands falling to his sides. "See, I suggest we give you to Osiris as a distraction while Caro brings the child to term in the sanctuary of other Seraphim."

Caro froze as the tension in the room thickened. She didn't need emotive abilities to tell how Sethios felt about that suggestion.

"You are more than welcome to try," he murmured darkly. "But first, tell me why you think Caro would want to be surrounded by beings who sent her here under false pretenses? They essentially lied to impregnate her with a child she may or may not have wanted."

"It was a logical assessment" was Gabriel's reply. But even she could hear the uncertainty in his response.

"Hmm, logic. Yes. Let's discuss logic. What rational part of you believes I will allow *my* child to be raised by anyone other than me and the mother?"

"I didn't say you would agree," Gabriel pointed out.

"Excellent. Then you'll understand why this isn't happening."

Gabriel arched a single blond brow. "You seem to be under the impression you have a choice in the matter."

"Enough," Caro rasped, unable to stand another minute of this bickering. Her insides were rioting, and she desperately craved a nap. "I can't do this right now."

Sethios tightened his hold on her. He'd held her this entire time without so much as a complaint. And that she hadn't demanded he release her was even more confusing. If she didn't know better, she'd suspect that she rather enjoyed being in his arms.

"What can I do, Caro?" He spoke low and close to her ear. "Do you want anything to eat? Drink? Do you want to lie down?"

She relaxed into his shoulder again with a sigh. "No food. I just want to rest. Then we can discuss what to do."

"All right, angel." He turned toward the hallway. "Stay, Gabriel."

Her son let out an uncharacteristic snort that caused her to frown.

"Don't make any decisions without me, Gabriel," she said, adding a stern note to her voice. "And don't fight Sethios." The words surprised her, mostly because she meant them.

"I appreciate your support, but I can handle him on my own, angel," Sethios murmured as he continued toward the bedrooms.

"I'll behave if he does," Gabriel called after them.

That would have to be good enough for now.

She rested against Sethios again and closed her eyes. His woodsy scent soothed her senses, calming her stomach. Odd.

"Your bed," she whispered. "Lay me there." Where she would be surrounded by him. That's what she needed.

He paused. "Are you sure?"

"Mm-hmm." She yawned as exhaustion rolled over her. "Just for a few hours."

"You're welcome to stay as long as you need, angel." He rotated, presumably in the direction of his quarters. She'd been staying in his version of a guest area at the end of the hall.

Comfort settled firmly over her as they entered his bedroom, and she knew immediately she'd made the right decision. Every part of her sighed in relief, including her soul, as he tucked her into blankets that smelled just like him.

"Thank you," she whispered.

He brushed a kiss against her forehead. "I'll be back to check on you in a bit."

She tried to nod, but her head felt too heavy. Her attempt at a verbal agreement lodged somewhere in her throat.

Too tired.

They would talk more later.

Until then, sleep.

CHAPTER TEN

Forging New Bonds

A baby.

Fuck.

Sethios had been able to hold it together while holding Caro in his arms, but the reality punched him in the face as soon as he returned to the living area.

Gabriel had relaxed into the oversized sofa, his legs sprawled in a deceptively relaxed manner. Only his eyes telegraphed the intelligence and lethality lurking behind his calm facade. Sethios recognized it well because the same proclivities existed inside himself.

"My mother trusts you," Gabriel said. "How did you manage to accomplish that in such a brief time?"

Sethios took the seat across from him, his stance open and ready for a fight should it become necessary. "Caro's body trusts me more than her mind." And certainly not her heart.

Her request to sleep in his bed had struck him hard in the chest. His instinct to do whatever she asked was certainly new.

Sethios only ever looked out for his own best interest, and occasionally a close friend. But when she gazed up at him with pain etched in her eyes, he'd have given up his soul to help her.

He rubbed his pec, conflicted by the response.

As much as he wanted to blame the knowledge of her pregnancy for the reaction, he couldn't. Because the notion to help her first occurred when he caught her in the kitchen. Panic unlike any he'd ever felt had slammed into his gut at the agony rippling through her expression.

"You care about her," Gabriel murmured, observing.

Sethios stared back at him. "Is this the part where you advise me to stay away from her? Tell me not to hurt her, or you'll kill me?" He could sense the power radiating off the Seraphim before him. It would be a fair fight, one Sethios might even lose.

"If you think that's needed, then you don't know my mother very well." There was a hint of pride in Gabriel's tone, but his expression remained artfully blank. "Caro is more than capable of killing you herself."

"So she keeps saying," Sethios mused.

"She's strategic. You would do well to remember that."

Amusement flighted through him despite the dire circumstances. Caro could probably harm him, if she ever truly tried. "I have no intention of ever hurting her."

If anything, he wanted to protect her. He'd warned her away from Osiris before he knew about the benefits of keeping her close. That behavior alone wasn't normal for Sethios, however, nothing about this situation struck him as ordinary.

"Giving you to Osiris as a distraction is the most practical option. That will grant Caro time to raise and prepare your child for whatever uprising the Fates feel your progeny will create." Gabriel spoke the words with an underlying hint of finality that didn't sit well with Sethios.

"So sacrifice myself for my family," he interpreted. "Except, according to Skye, I will be important to my father's downfall." Or that's what he inferred from Ezekiel. "It seems prudent we learn what she foresaw before jumping to any 'practical' solutions."

Gabriel steepled his fingers, his light green gaze thoughtful. Sethios could see the resemblance to Caro in his light hair and pale skin, but his face was too masculine to be considered angelic. He also possessed a lethal air that Caro lacked, one that grated on Sethios's nerves.

The warrior line, as Caro referred to it. Except her definition of their gifts reminded him more of strategy than physical combat.

She explained that hundreds of Seraphim family lines existed, all with varying powers. When he likened them to Hydraians and Ichorians, she continued to say that human genetics maintained similar coding to her Seraphim brethren. So it stood to reason that Hydraians and Ichorians would wake with unique gifts once his father's blood triggered their resurrection.

Magic.

Or science.

Either way, geneticists would have a field day researching the origins and how they morphed through rebirth.

"The Fates didn't mention your importance, but then again, they wouldn't." Gabriel's words pulled Sethios from his thoughts. "Especially if they are hoping to influence an outcome."

"Such as?"

"I'm not sure." Gabriel scratched his jaw. "They are playing with their own desired endgame, which is evident by not warning my mother of her purpose prior to her assignment. She's loyal and would have followed through if they issued an edict. That the council felt the need to withhold the directions suggests other players in place that have not yet been identified or discussed."

Okay, they would come back to the "additional players" part in a moment. Something else required clarification first. "Your council can demand procreation?"

Gabriel blinked. "Of course. Why do you think I exist? It was not by Caro's choosing but by the will of the Fates."

Sethios's eyebrows lifted. "She didn't want a child?"

"Whether she wanted one or not matters little. I was needed, therefore she created me with Adriel."

"Procreation by prophecy." Wow. And Sethios thought his father's commands were bad. "What if she didn't desire a child?"

"Desire is a human emotion that serves no true purpose in our world. We do what is needed when it serves a purpose."

Right. No wonder Gabriel looked so bored. "My purpose is to enjoy life."

"You are strongly influenced by humanity."

"And you're not?" Sethios couldn't help the sarcasm. The posturing from before certainly felt *emotional.*

"Correct. My gift is not tied to humanity, unlike, say, Zara's bloodline. Her talents would prove futile in the absence of humans since her gifts are based on emotions. Meanwhile, mine work regardless of humanity."

He frowned. "Zara?" That name had not come up in conversation with Caro.

"She's a member of the High Council and the leader of her line. Your father didn't teach you of our government structure?"

"No, but Caro mentioned each family has representation in the council." Considering there were hundreds of lines, Sethios imagined a giant auditorium filled with old, bored Seraphim discussing and issuing edicts. *They probably throw killer holiday parties.*

Gabriel studied him, a flicker of something drifting

through his gaze. "Yes, typically the oldest one in a state of awareness sits on the council."

"Awareness?" Sethios repeated. All these terms were completely foreign to him, at least in this context of conversation. His father had made it seem as if Seraphim were a dying breed, but Gabriel and Caro painted a picture of a well-structured society that existed *somewhere*.

"Eternity is daunting. Most Seraphim fall into a state of unconscious after a few millennia and awake only when they are needed."

"Like to procreate." Sethios meant it as a joke, but Gabriel took him seriously.

"Yes. Adriel awoke to create me."

"And he's on the council."

"Yes."

"Which makes you next in line." It was a guess considering everything Sethios had learned.

"Yes."

"What about Caro? Where does she fall?"

"My mother has several older generations above her, which is typical for one her age. I am a unique case, as most of the eldest Seraphim have no cause for breeding."

"So why were you needed?" Sethios asked, curious. "What purpose do you serve?"

"My fate has not yet come to fruition."

"Meaning you have no idea why your mother was forced to birth you. Fascinating." Sethios couldn't help the sarcasm in his voice. Their whole world was too contrived. None of them *lived*. No wonder the older Seraphim chose to nap for eternity. Sethios would, too, in their shoes.

"Our customs have served us well for several thousand years. We have no war, no famine, no pain. Can you say the same about your precious humans?"

Sethios snorted. "I wouldn't call them precious, and obviously I can't say the same, but I've lived a far more intriguing existence as a result. Stick around for a while and maybe you'll understand."

"I have no desire to remain here any longer than needed." Gabriel flicked his gaze toward the hallway and then back to Sethios. "That said, I'm interested in learning what your seer predicted. She won't be nearly as powerful as the Fates but may be more inclined to give us the whole version. When can we speak to her?"

"As soon as we figure out how to get around Osiris." Sethios grinned and stood. He needed a strong drink. Preferably a brandy. He found a bottle native to France and poured two healthy glasses. If the Seraphim didn't want any, he'd enjoy both.

Gabriel hadn't moved, nor had his expression changed, but he did accept the drink while saying, "Alcohol has no practical use."

"It tastes good. That's the only reason I require." Sethios settled back into his chair and sipped the amber liquid. It burned his throat in the most pleasurable of ways.

"Chocolate," Gabriel said after a long moment. "Caro may enjoy it."

"What purpose does it serve?"

"It tastes good," Gabriel parroted. "She may appreciate a little indulgence in her current state—something that would not be advised back home."

Was this an olive branch of sorts? "Noted."

Gabriel sipped his drink, almost as if to confirm their unspoken agreement to tolerate each other for the time being. After a few minutes, he set it to the side and folded one leg over the other. "Your comment earlier implies Osiris is guarding your seer. Tell me about his compound."

Sethios nearly laughed, then reconsidered his present company. If anyone could dance around the defense mechanisms, it was a Seraphim. He detailed the location and the variety of wards in place before diving into his suggestion. "You'll need Ezekiel because he'll know where Skye is being kept. My father likes to move her around."

"Who is Ezekiel?"

"My oldest friend. He has the ability to trace by blood,

making him a powerful tracker. My father has turned him into his personal hound dog by holding Skye hostage."

Gabriel cocked a brow. "How are the two related?"

"She's the love of his life." Or so his friend thought. Sethios tried to convince him to move on several times, but to no avail. "Ezekiel could easily tell my father to fuck off, but he stays for Skye."

"That's illogical."

"When you meet him, please tell him that." Because Sethios more than agreed. "He can help you locate Skye, but he will require some convincing. And my father's penchant for persuasion will make your negotiation tricky, as Ezekiel may be forced to report back details."

Although, if anyone could work around his father's antics, it was Ezekiel. The man excelled at word games and had centuries of practice finding loopholes.

"Your source sounds irrational and thereby unreliable." An astute deduction, but wrong.

"Perhaps, but he's your best bet." Ezekiel may have lost his head over a woman, but he was still quite useful. "He's also positively lethal. He's revered as the finest Nizari assassin in our history."

Gabriel rose one perfect eyebrow. "Should that mean something to me?"

"He hunts and kills fledglings, otherwise known as the offspring of Ichorians prior to being resurrected as Hydraians. Once he's tapped into a bloodline, it applies to any and all progeny." Sethios finished his drink and set it off to the side. "I suppose Seraphim don't pay much mind to Ichorian and Hydraian affairs."

"We were rather hoping you all would annihilate each other and save us all the task."

"Charming." The Seraphim must not have predicted the Treaty of 1747. Hell, they probably didn't even know about it. "I suggest you look for Ezekiel in New York City. I also strongly suggest you meet him before heading to my father's compound. Assuming you want to live."

"Osiris does not intimidate me."

Sethios shook his head in dismay. "I thought you Seraphim were supposed to be a logical lot. First Caro, now you... Do none of you realize what my father is capable of?"

Gabriel stared at him. "Why New York City?"

"Because Ezekiel has been helping my father with some project at the Catastrophic Relief Foundation. I'm pretty sure they are building super soldiers using Seraphim genetics, or that's what I've gathered, anyway. You might want to have a conversation with the Ichorian in charge—Jonathan Fitzgerald—about it while you're there."

"Seraphim genetics?"

"It's a guess, but my father is all about experimentation, and I've suspected for years that he's building an army. His recent partnership with Jonathan cannot be a coincidence."

Just the subtlest of tics in Gabriel's jaw indicated the first crack in his unemotional exterior. Sethios had clearly struck a nerve and perhaps even piqued his interest. His work here was done. Either the Seraphim would take his advice or he'd try to hand Sethios over to Osiris.

Emphasis on *try*.

He stood, needing to move. Or better yet... "I'm going to check on Caro."

"She's fine," Gabriel murmured. "I can sense her peace."

Right. Ethereal bond or whatever. "As I don't possess the same bond, I'll be checking for myself."

He'd left Caro in his bed at her request. If it were up to him, she'd live there. Naked. Pregnant or not, he still wanted her, and he had spent the last two weeks teasing her. He wanted her to beg him to fuck her, and she would. He just needed to up his game.

But first, they had a future to discuss.

Unreal.

Yet, he felt oddly okay with the notion.

It should have scared the shit out of him, but a child provided something new. An experience he'd not yet lived.

I'm going to be a father.

His lips curled with the thought. Then flattened at thoughts of his own maker. Did Osiris know? Was Skye, even at this minute, telling him about Sethios's future progeny?

He stopped in the doorway of his room and studied Caro. Her blonde hair popped against his black pillow, while the rest of her appeared soft and delicate beneath his silky sheets.

The mother of my future child.

His heart skipped a beat with the thought. On some level, he must have known. That explained his innate need to protect her, even when he barely knew her. Some hint of fate fucking with his instincts.

A sigh fell from her full lips as she burrowed more into his blankets.

So beautiful, yet deadly.

The perfect mate.

Mine, a dark part of him whispered. Perhaps not for eternity, but for now.

A piece of him grew inside of her—a future he would do *anything* to protect.

Chapter Eleven

Pleasurable Teamwork

Hot chocolate.

A sweet indulgence—one that would be frowned upon and ridiculed.

But Caro didn't care. Not when it tasted like pure heaven sliding down her throat. She cradled the mug against her chest, luxuriating in the warmth it brought her.

Seraphim didn't imbibe or eat anything without purpose. Her kind could survive on base nutrients alone, thereby not requiring luxuries such as chocolate. To indulge was considered impractical.

She took another sip and hid a grin. The decadent drink soothed her senses, which she determined to be a practical reason to enjoy it.

"Are you smiling?" Sethios asked, his head tilted in a

curious manner.

"No."

"And now you're lying?" He chuckled. "Fascinating."

She pulled the mug away from her mouth and settled it in her lap. "Where did Gabriel go?"

Caro expected him to still be here after her nap, rather instead it was just Sethios waiting for her with a steaming cup of hot chocolate. Her brain told her to refuse while her nose forced her acceptance, and oh, how she approved.

"To scout out Osiris's estate. He wanted to see the security measures for himself. I suspect he'll return once he realizes I was right about needing Ezekiel." Sethios didn't sound all that concerned. If anything, he appeared amused. "Can I get you anything else? Lunch, perhaps?"

Food didn't really appeal to her. "Is there more hot chocolate?"

His green eyes flickered with an emotion she couldn't name. "I can make more."

"I'd find that acceptable." *And may even like it.*

"Acceptable, hmm?" He stood and looked her over. "Well, if that's our term, then I find your dress *acceptable* as well."

"I was too hot for jeans," she explained. "This was a more practical option."

"Oh, on that, we agree." He winked and turned toward the kitchen.

She frowned, not understanding the flirtatious tone he used. Caro didn't much care for the short-skirted outfit, but she'd woken up in a state of such heat that she required something that allowed her skin to breathe.

Sethios had procured her a wardrobe shortly after they arrived, mostly consisting of jeans and shirts and a handful of summer dresses. She'd originally moved those to the back of her closet, having no desire to ever wear them. Alas, her body had required one today—a soft blue number that barely skimmed her knees.

So much for carrying my knives. The set Sethios had retrieved for her were adequate and currently in her nightstand. Her original plan of using them in retaliation against him seemed rather inconsequential in her current state.

She tucked her legs beneath her and finished her hot chocolate just in time for Sethios to bring her a new one in another mug. He took her used one without a word, then returned to stand before her.

"Should we talk about it?" he asked as he folded his arms.

Caro swallowed, feeling slightly intimidated by his height and the smolder in his eyes. She suspected that was the point. "What's there to talk about? I'm pregnant."

"Your initial reaction to the news suggested a conversation might be needed about the fate of our child." His emphasis on the word *our* did not escape her notice, nor did the flare in his nostrils. "Not to mention the whole decision being made for you by your kind. Gabriel might find that normal—hell, you might as well—but I do not. You are your own being; however, this discussion should include me."

"And what would you have me decide?" she asked, curious. Her mind was already set, but it'd be good to know what she'd be up against in this battle.

"I'm not interested in playing that game, angel." He kneeled before her, his hands going to the armrests of her chair. "It's your body and therefore ultimately your choice, but I will say this much. I've never wanted to be a father. It's a role I never had reason to contemplate, nor was it something I ever desired."

Her heart skipped a beat at the seriousness in his tone and the sincerity radiating from his eyes. His words were harsh, to the point, and exactly what she expected. Except for the part about it being her choice. Nothing in her life had ever really been up to her so much as up to Seraphim society.

"Caro," he continued, voice softening. "Even though the thought of not seeing this through kills a part of me, I'll endeavor to respect your preference." He pressed his palm to her stomach. "But a life I helped create is growing inside of you, and that's not something I could ever wish to destroy."

She blinked at him. "You want me to keep the baby." The words sounded foreign on her tongue, almost as if they'd been pulled out of her heart and forced into the air.

"I do, but I won't choose for you." He drew his thumb over her still-flat abdomen. "You believe this to be an abomination, I'm sure, but I view it as a miracle. It's something I never even considered dreaming about, and while I wish it were under different circumstances, I'll never regret it."

"Abomination or not, the fated line predicted it and apparently my council expected it."

A low growl emanated from him, confusing her. "Yes. We'll come back to that."

"Come back to what?"

"How fucked up that is," he said. "You might be used to having people issue verdicts on your behalf, but I'm not. They sent you here under false pretenses with the expectation of me planting my seed in you. How that doesn't infuriate you is beyond me."

"If it was fate, it was going to happen with or without their intervention."

"Leaving you no choice but to comply?" He shook his head. "I disagree. The intention of foresight is to have an opportunity to change it; otherwise, what's the point?"

"So you would prefer me to have refused and not created a child?"

"No, I wouldn't change anything about how we met or what ensued. But your elders played you, and I find that unacceptable."

"I see." She agreed that they should have been allowed to choose and that what her council did was wrong. "But I wouldn't change the outcome either. They must have known that."

"Did they?" Incredulity colored his features and tone. "That remains to be seen. We need to learn more about what they've predicted, as well as Skye, so we can better prepare ourselves. To protect our child, Caro."

He took the mug from her and set it aside, then grabbed her hands with his own. "Your son suggested sending me to Osiris, and if I thought that would protect you and our child, I'd think about it. But until we know more, that's not an option either of us can select. We need to be a team. That's the only way this is going to work."

Her breath caught in her throat at the intensity in his expression and in his eyes. He meant every word; of that, she had no doubt. Could she partner with this man? The one who essentially tricked her into bed that first night they met, promising her information that he later withheld?

He had granted her a semblance of freedom these last two weeks to do whatever she wanted. Caro had tried misting more than once, and he didn't stop her. No compulsion. She'd remained, mostly because she wanted to know more about Osiris's seer. Now that information mattered even more.

"A team," she repeated. "And if I would prefer to be in the sanctuary of my own people?"

"The same beings who sent you on a bogus errand with the intention of impregnating you with my child?" He smirked. "If that's your desire, then I'll either follow you or do what I can to protect you from here. But I would request—beg, even—that you wait to decide until after we know more about the prophecy."

Her lips threatened to curl. "Beg?" She might enjoy seeing that.

His gaze narrowed. "This is a serious conversation."

"Yes," she agreed. "You begging is very serious to me."

"Now you're teasing me," he growled, wrapping his hands around her wrists. "I'm trying to discuss something important, and you're smiling."

"I'm not smiling."

"Your eyes are smiling." He moved closer, sliding between her legs and lowering her palms to the armrests of the chair. "You know what I think?"

She bit her lip and shook her head. Though, she had an idea of where he might be headed given the devilish glint in his dark green eyes.

"I think you like me," he replied. "In fact, I think you might even find me useful during this pregnancy."

Her eyebrows rose. "In what way?"

"Hot chocolate, for one." His fingers slid from her wrists to her knees and started exploring upward beneath her dress. "I can also offer pleasure, something I hear pregnant women fancy."

"Both impractical."

"Are they?" His fingers slid up her thighs to her panties. "You were quite pale earlier, Caro. Yet, your cheeks are glowing healthily now. Why do you think that is?" The husky quality of his voice stroked over her, heightening her senses.

She cleared her throat. "My nap."

"Mmm." He traced the lace over her hips and continued inward toward her center. She dug her nails into the chair as his thumb unerringly found and pressed her pleasure point. "Your nap in my bed. Why did you choose that location, angel?"

Her lips formed several words that didn't escape clearly, or really at all.

This shouldn't be happening.

Not like you can get pregnant again, some unknown part of her whispered.

That's not the point.

She attempted to clamp her thighs closed, but his body blocked her.

"Having trouble?" he taunted.

"This isn't—"

"Practical," he finished for her. "Maybe. But I see it as a rational method of putting your body at ease. You deserve to be relaxed and comfortable, Caro. Let me help."

Yes…

Oh, she shouldn't.

But his thumb drew alluring circles against her, draining all the fight from her limbs.

Why stop him?

Because Seraphim weren't supposed to feel.

Seraphim weren't supposed to indulge in sweets either.

A moan slipped from her lips of its own accord, something he took as acceptance. Her panties disappeared with a snap, causing her to yelp in surprise.

"I'll replace them," he said, his mouth a breath away from her damp flesh.

He moves so fast…

Oh.

His tongue.

Yes.

There.

He seemed to know exactly what she craved without her uttering a single word or request. It was so wrong, this delirious sensation. And yet, so, so right.

She threaded her fingers through his hair and let her head fall back against the chair.

This man—this being—had changed a fundamental part of her. Her kind would be appalled. *She* should be appalled.

But how could she despise something that set her bloodstream on fire?

"Sethios," she managed to whisper, unable to breathe. Her heart lodged in her throat as her limbs locked in place. It felt like death. Or rebirth. She couldn't discern between the two. A precipice of greatness, shrouded in foreign sensation that teetered her right on the edge of a cliff.

And then she was flying, soaring through the clouds of ecstasy. Pins and needles mingled with shocks, scouring her soul and catapulting her high into the sky and beyond.

Totally different this time.

So much more intense.

Almost as if she'd held back during every orgasm with him before. And now that she'd accepted the inevitable, it took her to a state of being she didn't know existed.

"Again," she whispered as reality began to surface. "Please."

His green eyes grinned up at her. "Only because you asked so sweetly." He licked her deep, sending vibrations of lust through her veins. "You're mine, Caro."

She shook her head even as his claim latched onto her heart.

"You are, sweetheart," he insisted softly. "I warned you before, and I'll warn you again. I'm keeping you."

She wanted so badly to argue, but he silenced her protest with another hypnotizing move of his tongue.

"You have my vow of protection," he whispered, almost reverently. "My vow of partnership."

She shuddered as his words settled somewhere deep inside her, in a sacred place occupied by her soul. Such intensity, spoken as a heartfelt promise she couldn't deny.

They barely knew each other, and yet, that sacred place inside her recognized him. It bloomed and welcomed his pledge and reciprocated in kind.

Whatever the Fates had seen, whatever they believed could happen, had nothing on the power of the bond forming between them.

A part of Caro longed to hate Sethios, while the other part—the part she revered most—started to open to the possibility of a future. A forbidden blood bond.

"All right." She barely recognized the rasp in her voice or the words falling from her lips. But he needed to hear them. Just as she needed to say them. "We'll work together. As a team."

His gaze captured hers as he lifted his head from between her legs. "Then I'm yours, Caro. Whatever you need."

Her pulse raced as she nodded, agreeing to whatever pact they'd just formed between them. For the future of their child. For their future.

He cupped her face and brushed his lips over hers, finalizing their agreement. And she realized with a start that this was their first kiss.

Sethios had done unspeakable things to her body, but not this, making it a far more affectionate moment than everything else. Especially as his tongue gently entered her mouth to mate with hers.

The taste of her arousal infiltrated her senses, kicking up her heartrate even more, and the tenderness quickly turned to heat. Her thighs gripped his legs in a silent urge for more, and he grinned against her mouth.

"You want me to fuck you," he said.

"Yes."

"Tell me. Say the words."

"Fuck me." Caro didn't expect them to be so easy to say, but they fell from her mouth without preamble. Not because he demanded it, but because the crude request felt right. From what she knew of Sethios, he didn't make love; he fucked.

"Mmm, beautiful." He traced her lower lip with his tongue and lightly nipped her. "Sadly, I must decline."

Decline? "What?"

"This was for you," he murmured, his thumb wiping the moisture away from the edge of her mouth. "And you're not ready to beg me yet."

"I… What?" That made no logical sense.

"Delayed gratification, Caro. Trust me." He winked and pulled away, fixing her skirt as he went. "Now, I've had a delectable snack. What about you? Ready for lunch yet?"

"Lunch?" she repeated, utterly confused.

"Yes." He touched her hot chocolate mug with the back of his hand. "This appears to have cooled enough for you to drink now. You work on that, and I'll fix you something to eat."

She looked at the cup and then back at him. "I want sex, not food."

He grinned. "You have no idea how much I love hearing you say that."

"Then fuck me." Again it came out so easily. She might start using the word more liberally. It was quite fun.

"Oh, I intend to. But you need food first."

Caro gaped at him. He'd practically demanded she fornicate the first night they met. Now he was saying no? "I don't understand."

"You require nutrients, Caro. I'm feeding you."

"But—"

He pressed a finger to her lips. "Let me take care of you. Please."

Her eyes widened, startled by the sincerity radiating from him. The man was a living, breathing conundrum. One minute seducing, the next nurturing.

"The baby needs food," he added. "In case you were looking for a rational reason."

She blinked.

Right. Food facilitated growth.

"Then sex." *What is wrong with me?* She shouldn't be demanding this. But she wanted it. Badly. For no practical purpose other than to feel. *This man is going to be the death of me.*

"Don't worry, Caro. I'll give you what you need." His smile was positively wicked.

"Why do I think that's not what I'm requesting," she said slowly.

"Because you're intelligent, angel." He cupped her cheeks again and kissed her softly. "I do owe you another orgasm—since you asked so sweetly—and I intend to deliver." The words were a breath against her lips, followed by a punishing nip. "After you eat something. Immortal or not, our baby requires food."

"Our baby," she repeated. Why did that phrase spread warmth from her chest? "You really want to do this."

He pulled back to gaze into her eyes. "I won't lie to you, Caro. It's not something I've ever wished for, but I've not once considered the possibility of not having this child with you. Destiny or not, it feels too right."

She swallowed and nodded in understanding. Whether the Fates wanted this to happen or not remained a moot point in the presence of Caro's instinctual reactions to the life blossoming inside of her.

Protect.

Foster.

Cherish.

It was as if her soul had already vowed to do all those things without her conscious consent.

But as he said, it felt too right to resist.

"Okay, but this doesn't mean I like you," she whispered, not really meaning it.

He grinned against her lips. "I would hope not, angel. Otherwise, this partnership will be awfully boring."

"What if I prefer boring?"

"You don't." He drew his mouth along her cheek to her ear. "Because if you did, you wouldn't want to fuck me."

Words failed her. A denial would be a lie. Acceptance would only stroke his oversized ego. Remaining quiet seemed her only option, though that, of course, implied her agreement.

Sethios kissed her again, soundly, before standing. "Food first, angel. Then I'll pleasure you until you beg me to stop."

Well. If that's how he intended to treat her while pregnant, who was she to argue?

Her last pregnancy left her miserable and pained. Perhaps this time would be different with Sethios by her side.

Starting with more hot chocolate.

Part Two
Cursed Bonds

"An unknown power is surfacing. She will possess the strength and will to destroy us all unless certain measures are put in place to curb her inclinations. Sethios is key."

-Skye

CHAPTER TWELVE

Fresh Alliances

Gabriel leaned against the brick wall, gaze on the courtyard across from him. Beyond it stood a building he wanted to know everything about.

The headquarters of the Catastrophic Relief Foundation, otherwise known as the CRF.

It was a humanitarian organization led by millionaire Jonathan Fitzgerald—an Ichorian of poor talents. The public saw him as an enigma, being in his early twenties and owning a rather large company that sprouted out of nowhere. His son, one Thomas Fitzgerald, resided with Jonathan's supposed wife somewhere in upstate New York.

Supernatural powers were definitely at play here, but humans were naive. They believed the easiest lie rather than consider the impossible.

Gabriel crossed one jean-clad ankle over the other, waiting.

Sethios had given him a full description of Ezekiel. It was only a matter of time before the infamous assassin appeared. Especially as Gabriel had been anticipating his arrival for almost a week now.

His attempt at surveying Osiris's compound failed when he realized the Seraphim was using locator deciphers.

Tricky, talented, and intelligent.

A lethal combination for a sociopathic immortal with no sense of right or wrong.

It was no mystery to Gabriel why his council wanted this Seraphim removed. He'd created an army of minions with varying degrees of abilities, all with the sole purpose of protecting him in a fight. Not that any of them seemed too eager to act on their leader's behalf.

From what Gabriel had gathered, the Ichorians and Hydraians had no idea they existed because of Osiris's blood.

Fascinating, really.

And odd.

His endgame, while predictable, was shrouded in confusing layers. Why not claim his birthright and rule his kind? Why allow them to live in a state of ignorance? What point did it prove?

Gabriel wanted all the answers. Including to learn more about what lurked beyond the CRF gates.

He had considered, more than once, misting inside for a look around but didn't want to trigger any alarms. The runes surrounding the building rivaled those at Osiris's home, confirming Sethios's theory that the two men were working together.

But on what?

"You look like her," a voice said as a man materialized to the left. The man Gabriel had been waiting for. The newcomer's long black hair matched Sethios's description, as did the trademark leather jacket and pierced lip.

"Ezekiel," Gabriel replied, not missing a beat.

"Seraphim." The astute gleam in the Ichorian's gold-flecked gaze suggested intelligence and cunning, something Gabriel would need to keep in mind during their negotiations. "Or I assume that's what you are since I can't sense your origin."

He ignored the assessment. Explaining his gift for tracking evasion wasn't the purpose for this meeting. "I wish to speak with your seer."

Ezekiel quirked a brow. "My seer?"

"Yes. The one Osiris uses to keep you on a leash." Gabriel still didn't understand how that worked. The being standing before him radiated power. He'd even been able to somewhat surprise Gabriel with his unexpected appearing act. Why would someone with such ability bother working for a Seraphim like Osiris? Further proof that emotions were a waste of energy and common sense.

"You've been talking to Sethios," Ezekiel surmised. "I don't suppose you'll tell me how to find him?"

"No." Gabriel vowed to protect Caro, which included safeguarding Sethios. For the moment, anyway.

"Good." The Ichorian grinned. "I would hate to have to relay any details to Osiris."

"Compulsion?"

"Always."

Gabriel nodded, understanding.

Osiris had likely weaved some sort of persuasion into Ezekiel to ask about Sethios's whereabouts, as well as a need to relay any information pertaining to his location back to the master Seraphim. They would need to tread carefully in this conversation. Any little detail could trigger a compulsion to report back to Osiris.

"I'm here of my own accord. I require information, and it's my understanding your seer has that information."

"And you wish me to help you reach her."

"Yes."

Ezekiel's gaze moved over Gabriel in a way that spoke

of strategy and planning.

He's deciding if I can be useful to him.

Gabriel returned the favor in kind before focusing on the CRF headquarters again. "What are Osiris and Jonathan working on together?"

"Atrocities," Ezekiel replied as he followed his stare. "Osiris wants a mate for breeding purposes, and a potential candidate was birthed just last week. Apparently, I am to be her guard dog."

"In exchange for continued access to your seer."

"Indeed." Ezekiel refocused on Gabriel. "Why can't I sense you?"

"Genetics." He pushed off the wall to straighten to his full height, only an inch or so above the Ichorian. "It's a family trait."

"Intriguing. I'm guessing that is related to why I can't find Sethios. Don't confirm; just tell him to keep doing what he's doing. Osiris is positively furious." Ezekiel sounded delighted and even grinned. "I think you might be useful to me, Seraphim."

"I don't work for anyone."

"A partnership, then."

"I don't work *with* anyone either."

"I see." The light dimmed in Ezekiel's gaze, darkening his irises to a near black. "In that case, you don't need me, do you?"

Well played, Ichorian. Well played.

"What are you requesting in return for your assistance?" Gabriel didn't want to beat around the bush or continue this posturing game. He wanted to arrive at the point and be done with all the prophecy business.

Then he might return to take a second look at the CRF.

"I'm not sure yet. It depends on how good you are, Stark."

Gabriel frowned. "Stark?"

"Consider it a nickname. Keeps me from knowing your real identity and it suits you." The Ichorian winked. "I assume you've already tried to enter Osiris's estate and failed?"

"Entering was not my issue so much as locating my target."

"And what do you intend to do with your 'target'?"

"Request a prophecy. Nothing more. Nothing less."

Ezekiel eyed him in a considering manner. "I will require to be there, and if you try anything, you'll regret it."

"Threats are unnecessary," Gabriel replied flatly. "I'm only interested in her vision and conveying the details to an interested party." He purposely withheld Sethios's and Caro's names but knew the Ichorian understood when his lips curled.

"Brilliant. I'll need some time to work out the details." He tucked his hands into his leather jacket and cocked his head curiously to the side. "I don't suppose you fancy a drink? There's a place down the street with great scotch. You might even find it… compelling."

A hint of some kind, or perhaps a warning.

Gabriel's mission was to find the seer. Ezekiel intended to either aid him in that or lead him on an errand. Only one way to find out. "I've nothing better to do."

The Ichorian grinned. "Excellent. Perhaps chat with me as if that was our expected plan all along?"

Ah, we're being watched. "Of course."

"Brilliant." He nodded with his head in the direction for them to walk by the CRF. As they neared the gates, Ezekiel asked, "Are you still fucking that witch from London?"

Gabriel fought a grimace and played along. "The one with the fiery red hair?"

"Yeah. Can't remember her name. Tabby?"

"Abby." Gabriel couldn't force a warm reply but tried for a grin that felt foreign on his lips. The expression Ezekiel gave him told him to stop trying. "We're not seeing each other anymore."

He raised his brows. "I can tell by that look." Ezekiel smirked as they turned the corner. "Never know who might be listening."

"And now?"

"We're good. Something tells me you won't raise any red flags."

A thought nagged at Gabriel. "How did you recognize me?" He should have asked earlier, but he'd been preoccupied with finally completing his first step of the mission.

Ezekiel smiled fondly. "Skye told me where to trace but didn't tell me why. Then your light hair reminded me of the last Seraphim I briefly met, so I assumed you were who Skye sent me to meet."

That implied the Ichorian met with the seer alone, perhaps often. Sethios had stated Ezekiel was only granted one day a year with her in return for obedience. It seemed that might not be completely accurate.

Gabriel pocketed the detail for later investigation.

Ezekiel paused outside the entrance of a bar, hand on the door. "Meet me here in five days. I'll provide an update."

Gabriel studied the name and location. "Done."

"Cheers." He wandered inside and went straight for a man sitting on a stool. "Dear Owen. You and I need to—"

The door closed on whatever Ezekiel had been saying. Gabriel considered entering—if anything, to see why the dark-skinned man by the counter had turned an unfavorable shade of green—but decided it wasn't his business.

Curiosity served no purpose. Especially where Ichorian politics were involved.

Because the immortal inside was a Hydraian, sitting on notorious Ichorian turf.

An unintelligent choice considering the laws governing their kinds.

Gabriel didn't understand any of it. If Osiris would just take ownership of his minions, none of the bickering would be needed. Though, it seemed that was precisely what Osiris wanted—chaos.

One day Gabriel would seek to understand it.

Until then, he had a sibling to learn more about.

He misted home, to the lands on Earth shrouded in protection runes. Humans didn't know these areas existed, and the Seraphim preferred to keep it that way.

Time for another discussion with the seers. He doubted they would be any more forthcoming, but it was worth a shot.

If anything, he could compare their talents to those of the one named Skye.

Perhaps she would be more powerful than he expected.

Or lack any real means at all.

Only experience would tell.

CHAPTER THIRTEEN

Colorful Words

Caro woke to a headache.

It spiked behind her eyes, blurring her vision of the ceiling.

She moaned softly to herself, frustrated. This pregnancy was leagues better than her first one, but every time she tried to do something alone—like sleep—the pain returned tenfold.

Her body seemed to require Sethios's presence.

But she'd stalked off to her bedroom because she meant to punish him for not giving her what she wanted.

Sex.

He'd withheld it for weeks now. Oh, he pleasured her nearly every day—usually with his mouth—but he refused to do anything else. Almost as if he was afraid to break her.

She growled.

The man was driving her positively wild. Emotions unlike any she'd ever experienced overwhelmed her every thought.

Fury, lust, frustration.

He'd turned her into a Seraphim with feelings.

She didn't care for it. Nor did she appreciate the ache between her thighs or the throbbing in her head.

Caro sighed. She knew the cure to all her ails. It lay a few feet away in the other room in the form of male perfection.

"Fuzz," she muttered. "Fuzz, fuzz, fuzz."

Fuck, her mind supplied.

"That too."

She rested a palm over her fluttering abdomen. The bump was small, but there—an indication that this pregnancy would fall under a similar timeline to her last one. That meant they might have a baby in five weeks or so. Two-month gestational periods were fairly standard for Seraphim.

Interesting how reproducing took specific requirements and a perfect genetic match, but the actual birth rushed right along upon procreation.

The pounding in her head increased, forcing her from the bed. She nearly ran into the hallway wall as she padded toward Sethios's room. This had become their routine. She tried to stay away from him and ended up beside him by morning.

So she wasn't surprised when he lifted his arm in welcome upon hearing his door open. "Come here, sweetheart," he murmured softly.

Caro slid beneath the covers and immediately felt the relief of his warmth washing over her. She curled into him, luxuriating in his calming scent and strength.

Safe, her body seemed to whisper.

He rubbed her side in soothing circles as he pulled her impossibly closer and pressed his lips to her temple.

"Better?" he whispered.

"Yes."

"Good."

His lack of a shirt and pants added to the intimacy of the moment. After the first night she climbed in with him and found him naked, he'd started wearing boxers to bed, something she both appreciated and disliked.

Caro rather enjoyed him in the nude.

The man was perfectly proportioned in every way.

Her lips curved as she pictured him—muscular, hard, and so very delicious. She wanted to lick every inch of him and taste him the way he did her.

Oh, yes…

She squirmed as heat spread from her center to each limb. Her fingers tingled with the need to explore him, while her tongue desired something far more decadent.

What is wrong with me? Never in her existence had she yearned for such a thing.

It was as if Sethios had flipped a hormonal switch inside of her, and she couldn't figure out how to turn it off.

At least her headache was gone.

Caro focused on her breathing, matching Sethios's calming pattern. His body was so relaxed against hers that it lulled her into an addicting sense of comfort.

Her heart slowed. Her muscles unwound. Potential dreams scattered through her mind.

And crashed as a lethal presence stung her senses.

She didn't move. Didn't react outwardly. But she *felt* it.

Something cruel—an aura that didn't belong.

How is that possible?

Doesn't matter. Just run.

Sethios remained behind her, unaffected, yet she sensed his alertness.

He knows.

And if he doesn't? her nerves asked, fraying at the ends.

No. She couldn't think about that now.

They needed to move, and quickly.

But, God, if she was wrong…

She engaged her instincts and misted them to their backup-plan location—a random home in the middle of Montana. Sethios's arms closed around her as his mouth latched onto her neck, pulling her essence in quick, violent pulls.

Caro cried out at the invasion but understood the purpose and need. Her gift had worn off, allowing an evil presence to find them.

Osiris.

Sethios finished as fast as he began and pressed his forehead to her shoulder, his inhale harsh against her skin. "Fuck," he breathed. "Too fucking close."

"How did he find us?"

He shook his head, either because he didn't know or because he couldn't formulate a response yet. Her misting seemed to weaken him, perhaps because it went against the natural order to carry him with her. He wasn't a Seraphim. Not completely, anyway.

Caro remained alert, waiting for the evil aura to appear again, but silence surrounded them. That could be deceiving, however, as she shouldn't have been able to feel Osiris's misting approach to begin with. Yet, somehow, she did.

My abilities are shifting.

Why?

That didn't happen when she birthed Gabriel. Why would this new child be any different?

Sethios.

The thought clicked on a gasp. "I sensed him because your blood is inside me. In the child." She blinked, shocked by the obvious connection. "Our baby saved us."

That was the mark of a great power. Unnatural. Amazing. Mind-blowing.

"An innate instinct to protect," he whispered, his head still buried in her shoulder. "You misted us before he even stepped into the bedroom."

"Did he follow?"

Sethios shook his head. "I don't feel him."

She waited, watching and searching for even the tiniest change of energy.

The home remained utterly quiet, but outside, the sun was setting.

Time difference.

Right.

Her limbs shook as the adrenaline fled her system in a rush, and Sethios's arms were all that held her upright. Despite his obviously weakened state, he managed to lift her and carry her into what appeared to be an oversized living area. The lack of dust suggested he visited often, or, more likely, someone maintained the home in his absence.

Sethios settled into the closest chair with her in his lap and buried his head in her neck once more. "Thank you," he whispered.

Her brow furrowed. "For what?"

"Taking me with you."

His words struck her right in the heart. Not for a moment had she considered leaving him behind. She could have easily misted without him, even with him holding her, but she'd been utterly focused on their connection to ensure he did come with her.

She blinked.

What would have happened if she hadn't joined him in bed? If she had stayed in her own room and sensed the presence from there? Picking someone up mid-mist wasn't possible. If Osiris arrived while they were separated, she'd have no choice but to leave Sethios behind.

Unless they formed a proper blood bond. That would connect them on a level so deep that she'd be able to find him anywhere. Assuming she was able and coherent, of course.

Could she consider such a connection? Yes.

Should she? No.

They were about to have a child together, but neither of

them knew what the future held. Their partnership was tentative, at least for now.

But perhaps once they knew more—knew each other better—they could discuss a blood bond.

Maybe.

Until then, they needed to make certain provisions in case Osiris found them again.

"You need to drink from me at least twice a day, and we will remain within two feet of each other going forward." There. That would cover it.

Sethios chuckled. "Yeah? Does that include showering together, angel?"

"Yes. You must remain within arm's reach of me to be misted, or we risk my having to leave you behind."

"Chaining us together already?" He did not appear to be taking her seriously. "And I haven't even proposed yet."

She turned in his lap to level him with a glower. "Do you understand that had I been in my room when he arrived, I would have been forced to leave you behind?"

Some of his amusement faded as he held her gaze. "And that would bother you?"

"Yes." What a ridiculous question. "Of course it would."

A fire lit his green irises. "You took me with you because you wanted to."

"You didn't compel me, if that's what you mean." She could sense his persuasion, and he hadn't used it on her in weeks.

"Caro." He threaded his fingers through her hair and pulled her face close to his. "You saved me tonight. Because you wanted to."

"Why do you seem startled by that?"

"It shows you care."

She scoffed at that. "Caring is a human trait."

"It's a natural instinct," he fired back. "For some."

"Fine. Maybe. I don't know. All I could think about when I felt Osiris's presence was misting us both out of there, and I was terrified you wouldn't be awake enough to hold on to me." She stopped talking and nibbled her lip. If he hadn't been aware…

His mouth captured hers in a violent move that scrambled all her thoughts.

I… Oh.

Okay.

More.

Sethios had kissed her before, but not like this.

He practically devoured her, much in the same way he did… down there.

Mouth fucking, she realized. But with more heat and emotion, and a carnality that left her breathless.

His hands fell to her hips. In a move as quick as lightning, he had her straddling his lap with her sex pressed intimately to his and restarted their kiss before she could properly inhale.

Heat mingled with sensation throughout her body, stirring a fire deep inside. She had no idea an embrace could be so enlightening. So inspiring. So *real.*

Her nails dug into his bare shoulders as his tongue dominated hers. This was no civil mating, but a claiming that required her submission. And she couldn't refuse him. She doubted she ever could.

What is happening to me?

Three weeks ago, she would have resisted this compulsion to do whatever Sethios wanted. But now? She couldn't give him enough.

Her shirt disappeared over her head, followed by her sanity. His teeth scraped against her neck, her collarbone, and down to her breasts. She arched into him on a moan and clung to his biceps.

Sethios stood with her legs wrapped around his waist and started moving blindly through the home. When her back hit a soft mattress, she sighed in contentment.

"How many places do you own?" Because clearly, this house belonged to him.

"Several." He pulled off her pajama bottoms and

panties. "I'm going to pleasure you until morning, Caro."

She frowned at that. "You mean fuck me until morning."

He grinned as he kneeled between her legs. "With my mouth, yes."

She tried to close her thighs, but his hands stopped her. "Sethios," she growled.

"Yes, Caro?"

"I don't want your mouth. I want *you*." She emphasized by squeezing him with her legs.

His eyes glittered deviously. "What part of me?"

"You're going to make me say it?"

"Absolutely, I am."

She gritted her teeth. First it was *fuck*. Now he wanted another word she never had cause to use. But if it worked, it would so be worth the reward. "I want your cock, Sethios."

He grinned. "Where?"

"In me."

He cocked a brow. "Specifically, Caro. Because I count three ways to fuck you with my cock, and if I have it my way, I'll be exploring each option. Thoroughly."

Vulgar man. "I want your cock in my…" She swallowed, unable to say the crass term he wanted. "Center."

He chuckled and shook his head slowly. "Oh, angel. So close."

"Sethios." It came out as a growl. "You know what I want. Stop torturing me and pleasure me with your cock, or I swear, I will mist you to the middle of the Atlantic Ocean and drop you for a nice, long swim." Then she would use her wings to fly above the water while he fought the waves.

"I'd enjoy doing that right about now as well," said a flat male voice from the doorway, startling them both. "Or, better yet, I'll drop him in the middle of an active volcano."

CHAPTER FOURTEEN

Fuck. Fate.

"Gabriel," Caro breathed, her face turning a pretty shade of pink.

Embarrassment. Interesting. It seemed the Seraphim had begun embracing her emotions. Too bad Sethios couldn't explore it further. Maybe later. After her son left.

"Knocking isn't a formality where you're from?" Sethios asked casually as he moved over Caro, pulling a blanket along the way to cover her very naked body.

"No," came the flat reply from the doorway.

"How are you here?" Caro asked, her expression mellowing into stoicism as she held the comforter against her bare breasts.

"Sethios provided me with this address last week as an alternative location." Gabriel flipped on the lights and leaned against the doorjamb. "As Osiris and two of his minions were occupying the Paris condo when I arrived, I assumed that meant you both had left."

"Did he see you?" Sethios wondered. It didn't really matter since Gabriel couldn't easily be followed, just like his mother, but it would be good to keep the Seraphim anonymous so he could continue meeting with Ezekiel.

"No. I suspected something wasn't right before I appeared, likely a result of the bloodline." Gabriel eyed his mother. "You were distressed."

"Because Osiris found us," she replied.

The Seraphim's gaze narrowed slightly. "Of course." His tone held a touch of disbelief, but he didn't press it. "In any case, I misted a block away and wandered into the building in human form. He didn't notice me."

Sethios relaxed against the headboard, beside Caro, content with Gabriel's news. "Do you have an update?"

"Yes and no. The fated line is still withholding details— not that they will admit it—but I sense their hesitation. There is something they do not wish for us to know but have confirmed your progeny will possess unspeakable power. And have also insinuated the need to raise the child among Seraphim, not humans."

"Your tone suggests you disagree," Sethios noted. "Why?"

Gabriel blinked at him. "Seraphim do not speak in tones."

"And now you're avoiding my question."

"I refuse to draw conclusions from conjecture," Gabriel replied simply. "Therefore, it is not about disagreement but about uncertainty. They are speaking in riddles meant to provoke thought, not truth."

"Prophecies are like that." Or, at least, all the ones Sethios had heard were, anyway. "Why would they hide details?"

"Because they wish to shape the future." Gabriel pushed off the door to enter the room. "That is why they sent my mother here under false pretenses rather than provide her with the knowledge of foresight. They desired your mating and must have felt forewarning her would have deterred her." His light green eyes fell to his mother. "Do you agree?"

"Yes." No hesitation from Caro. "But that's the value of predicting the future—the ability to change it. That they did not wish for me to be aware of their vision proves their need to ensure it happened."

Gabriel stopped beside the bed and tucked his hands into his leather jacket. "Which is why I want the whole prophecy, not pieces of it. They say you need to raise the child among Seraphim, but they won't say why. While I can imagine several practical purposes, I suspect there is a specific reason for the requirement."

Sethios's eyebrows slid upward. "They are requiring we raise our child among your kind?"

"No." Gabriel met his gaze. "They are requiring *Caro* to raise her child among our kind."

"And me?" Sethios didn't bother hiding his sarcasm. "What would they like me to do?"

Gabriel shrugged. "You were not mentioned."

"Fascinating," he replied. "So I'm free to do whatever I want." Just as he always did. Good thing, too, because his choice would be to follow Caro and be a part of their child's life. "I hope you have a big bed, angel. As you know, I like to sprawl out when I sleep."

She gaped at him. "Excuse me?"

"I'll be moving in." He placed his palm over her abdomen. "This is my baby too. Your seers can fuck right off."

Her lips formed a cute little "O."

"You're surprised." He lifted his hand to cup her face. "What did you expect me to do?"

"I… I didn't expect anything." She swallowed visibly. "I hadn't considered it."

"Well, now you don't have to, because I'm not going anywhere, Caro."

Emotion brightened her gaze, electrifying her features.

God, he found her beautiful before, but she appeared positively radiant now. Passion and adoration were two sentiments she needed to display more often. He would endeavor to spark those reactions from her whenever possible.

Sethios studied her curving lips and felt his mimicking the action.

So gorgeous.

Sweet.

Intelligent.

Mine.

"I would make arrangements here in Montana," Gabriel said, interrupting the moment. "It's quiet, sparsely populated, and easy to protect. I'm guessing Osiris found you in Paris through facial recognition technology, but I will confirm with Ezekiel when I meet him tomorrow."

Sethios switched his focus to the Seraphim. "I assumed Ezekiel traced my father to the condo."

Gabriel shook his head. "He wasn't there, which leads me to believe Osiris located you via other means. Large cities are littered with surveillance equipment, and while our blood makes us untraceable, it does not shadow our facial features."

"Meaning he likely located me on one of my various trips outside." He hadn't bothered disguising his features, something he would reconsider moving forward. Although, it shouldn't be needed in this area of Montana.

Most of the properties around Seeley Lake were vacation homes owned by the wealthy or houses passed down to family members. That meant infrequent visitors and constantly changing faces.

And the nearest city was ninety minutes away.

"Staying here is perfect," Sethios murmured, agreeing with Gabriel's assessment. "At least until we know more."

"Good." Caro laid her head against his shoulder and sighed with contentment. "I like it here."

"Do you?" He chuckled as she nodded. "We just arrived."

"The air is clean," she murmured, yawning.

"It reminds her of home," Gabriel added softly. "Take her outside during the sunrise. She'll appreciate it." The Seraphim took a step backward. "I'll be in touch soon." He didn't wait for a reply or acknowledgment before he vanished.

"For one who strives for stoicism, your son certainly displays odd bouts of emotion," Sethios mused. Gabriel kept laying hints on how to appease Caro, as if he wanted to ensure her happiness. That spoke of a nurturing bond, something that required sentiment.

"It's our bloodline," she replied. "We've spent too much time around humans."

"Your son said your line isn't tied to humanity."

"Not directly, no. But we've spent thousands of years interacting with them." She lifted her head to gaze at him. "Our ability to conceal our auras marks us as prominent messengers. We are the ones chosen to deliver news and warnings to humans; it's why humanity commonly refers to us as guardian angels."

His eyebrows rose. "You warn humans?"

"Of course. At least, those who show promise." She smiled. "It's not frequent by any means, but we've been known to interfere on occasion. Well, not me or Gabriel specifically, but our ancestors."

Fascinating. There was still so much Sethios didn't understand about her kind and their impact on the world. "So Gabriel shares your line and his father's gift for war, but what about you? What is your second line?"

"My mother has the gift to heal any ailment, but it has never stirred inside of me. That happens sometimes, where bloodlines remain dormant and never prosper." Her gaze took on a faraway glint.

"The seers predicted I would need it one day," she continued. "That's why my mother was chosen to birth me, but I've yet to require a need for it. Nor have I ever felt a link to that ability, so they likely prophesied incorrectly, or the reason never came to fruition."

"Or it has something to do with our future child," Sethios murmured. "Because it would pass to her, yes?"

Caro considered, her brow furrowing. "Potentially, but with your father's bloodline running prominently through you, I imagine those gifts will trump mine. Osiris is the Seraphim of Life and Resurrection. He's considered one of the most powerful beings in our history."

"What about his gift for persuasion?" Caro kept mentioning resurrection while ignoring the far more lethal ability his father exuded. "Is that from a different line?" He knew nothing about his grandparents, thanks to his maker's cryptic nature.

Caro blinked at him. "Osiris can resurrect any breathing being—not just humans—and his blood is one of the ancient lines. It's not about compulsion so much as his *will*. If he desires something to happen, he can force it."

Sethios frowned. "Right, but how does that tie to resurrection?"

"He controls life," she replied. "While he is known for his ability to resurrect, his line controls all facets of the life cycle. As do you."

She said it so casually, as if that sort of power wasn't a mind-blowing revelation.

Oh, you control life.

Good to know.

"Does that mean my father can kill a Seraphim?"

"Hypothetically, yes. And there are rumors that he has, which is what provoked his exile. However, I wasn't alive when the council issued their edict, so it is all conjecture."

"Knowing what I do about my father, I'd say it's likely

true."

"I agree," she murmured.

"So my grandparents must be even more powerful, right? Can they be used to control Osiris?"

She stared at him as if he'd said something completely insane. "Your father is the eldest of his line. There is no one above him, Sethios. He just *is*."

Now it was his turn to gape at her. "How was he created?"

"The ancient ones came to be by unknown means, presumably by the gods. Osiris and Gabriel's father, Adriel, are original Seraphim. There are no beings above them. That's part of why I believe the council allowed Osiris so much free rein—they do not wish to destroy an ancient being. Or perhaps, they can't."

"But Skye prophesied his demise."

"Through our child," she replied. "Yes."

His heart froze as the implications of it all weighed over his spirit and mind. "Your seers seek to use our progeny. That's why they want you to raise the child among them— so they can control the future."

Her responding expression didn't register shock or dismay, suggesting she'd already drawn the same conclusion.

"They plan to use our baby to either defeat Osiris or to prevent some alternate outcome," he added, his voice thickening with a foreign emotion—the need to protect. "We can't allow that, Caro. What kind of life would it be?"

"A Seraphim existence."

"A tortured one." He pulled away from the headboard to angle his body toward hers. "Our child will not be a puppet, Caro. I've lived far too long beneath a puppet master to allow such a fate." The vehemence in his words surprised him. He hadn't realized how passionate he was about their child's future until he voiced his feelings.

His gaze fell to her blanket-covered abdomen, then flicked back up to her face. A demand entered his mouth but halted at the sight of her tears.

"Caro," he breathed, concern replacing his rage.

She pressed a hand to his bare chest as he moved toward her.

"It's just..." A shudder visibly rocked her, deepening his worry for her. "I feel the same way, Sethios. It goes against everything I am, everything I've been bred to believe, but my instincts are telling me the same thing. We can't let the seers decide her future."

"Her?" Sethios repeated.

Caro blinked. "I... I don't know where that came from. It just... I think we're having a girl."

"Can you know for sure?" There was technology available to humans, but would they work on a Seraphim?

She palmed her stomach and smiled. "I don't want to spoil it, and we'll know in a few weeks anyway."

"I still can't get over that," he admitted. When Caro told him the gestational period was about one week to one human month, he couldn't believe it. But she was showing already, and her escalated symptoms only added to the veracity of their situation. "Will she"—*oh, shit, a girl?*—"age differently?" The words rasped in his throat.

He already accepted his role as a father, but somehow this conversation made it all the more real.

I'm going to be a dad.

"Differently from humans?" Caro guessed.

He nodded since his mouth only seemed to want to say one word: *fuck.*

"Seraphim mature similarly until they cease aging. When did you stop changing?"

Sethios assumed she meant changes to his physical appearance. "I seemed to stop aging when I reached twenty-five or so." Unlike Hydraians, he didn't require death to be resurrected, though he suspected his father wanted to kill him, just for the hell of it, on more than one occasion.

"And your powers grew with you?"

"I suppose, but I could always compel." Even at a young

age, he could force those around him to do exactly what he wanted without whispering a word. "But my other ability—to borrow talents—didn't surface until later." It wasn't nearly as strong as his persuasion, but it helped hide his birthright.

"Seraphim grow into their talents as well. Our daughter will have one prominent ability with birth—either her aura concealment or your gift for life. Then she'll continue to cultivate her skills throughout her first twenty-five years or so."

"Will she be able to mist and form wings?" he wondered. "Because I can't."

"I'm not sure." She frowned. "I hope she can."

He hoped she could as well. "So she'll age like a human."

"Yes. Seraphim are most vulnerable in their youth, which is why we need to take measures to protect her and allow her to foster her gifts."

"Montana is more secluded than other areas of this country, or do you have another location in mind?"

"Here feels right," she murmured. "I feel... content."

"Then we'll stay here."

"Yes." She trailed her fingers up his chest to his neck and curled her palm around his nape. "Together."

"I've never been one for monogamy, Caro," he admitted. "Nor have I ever desired it." The words—thought a thousand times before—sounded wrong, even to his own ears, as he said them. *Nor have I ever desired it... until you.*

Well, that's certainly new.

Her eyes narrowed. "Seraphim do not take mates."

He cleared his throat, focusing on her statement instead of the monogamous inclinations rolling around in his head. "Then what are you requesting of me?"

Her eyebrows curved downward as she considered. "A partnership. I want us to work together to keep our daughter safe."

"That I can do." He threaded his fingers through her hair to hold her in place when she attempted to pull away.

"What else?"

Her gaze dropped to his lips, then slowly slid upward. "Sex."

His lips quirked upward. "Now? Or ongoing?"

"Both."

"Exclusively?" he asked, curious as to where she saw this going. Because the notion of her bedding another man did not agree with him. Nor did he possess the desire to fuck anyone other than Caro. *Such a fascinating development.*

"Maybe." She pressed him back into the mattress and straddled his hips. The blanket fell from her naked body, giving him a view he could definitely admire for eternity. "For now. Yes."

Sethios didn't do commitment, but Caro tempted him in a way few others ever had. Hell, the woman had outperformed all his former conquests in the bedroom *and* proven she could handle his darker desires. Why would he give that up?

"For now." He reaffirmed his grip in her hair and used it to guide her downward so her breasts touched his chest. "To be renegotiated at a later time."

She nodded, her lips brushing his. "Yes. When we decide a change is needed."

"Okay." He slid his hand to the back of her neck and squeezed. "Are you ready to beg me, sweetheart?"

"I'm ready for you to fuck me with your cock," she replied, her legs squeezing his upper thighs. "You mentioned three methods. Teach me all of them."

His brows rose. "Feeling adventurous?"

"Stop teasing and fuck me, Sethios. Now."

God, with a mouth like that? Yeah, he might keep her for eternity after all.

"As you wish, darling."

CHAPTER FIFTEEN

A New Partnership

Gabriel sipped the brandy the bartender poured for him and determined Sethios's brand from a few weeks ago was superior to this one. It still tasted better than all the drinks offered at home.

Seraphim didn't value flavor, something Gabriel felt needed to change. In addition to several other customs, like allowing the fated line the ability to determine the future of every living being.

He downed the rest of his drink and signaled for another just as Ezekiel wandered inside.

"See, I knew I liked you," the Ichorian said as he took a seat beside him. "I'll have one as well, love." The redhead behind the bar grinned at them and grabbed two glasses.

Ezekiel appeared exactly the same as the first time they

met, in a black leather jacket, jeans, long hair falling over his shoulders, and a lip ring. Except now he had tattoos on his hands. "Why did you color your knuckles?"

"Boredom," he replied. "It heals in about six hours, making it only temporary, so I have to do it all over again if I want to maintain it."

"That sounds illogical."

"I like pain."

"Clearly." Because his skin looked positively angry at him for brutalizing it. "Perhaps you should try inflicting it on someone else instead." Ezekiel struck him as the sadist type.

"Oh, now, you see, I would; alas, I'm rather committed to Skye."

And too much information. "I didn't mean during fornication."

"Are you condoning murder?"

"If the punishment suits the crime." Gabriel didn't shy away from a little violence. Some people deserved to be hurt. Like Osiris.

"Yes, we are going to make great partners indeed," the Ichorian beamed as he accepted a glass from the bartender. "Cheers." He rose the amber liquid in Gabriel's direction.

"Partners?" he repeated. Did Gabriel not say last time they were together that he preferred to work alone?

"To partners," Ezekiel said, clinking their drinks together and completely missing the question in his voice. Or perhaps ignoring it.

"And what are we partnering on, exactly?"

"The future of humanity." Ezekiel downed his brandy in one swallow before slamming it on the counter. "Drink up, Stark. We need to get moving."

Gabriel bristled at the nickname but did as the Ichorian requested. He tossed a few large bills on the counter for the redhead. "You can keep the change."

Without a backward glance, he followed Ezekiel out the door. "She totally would have fucked you, had you asked," the Ichorian informed.

"Who?"

"The bartender."

"Why?"

Ezekiel's ebony gaze danced over him. "It's true, then—what they say about Seraphim and sex?"

"Depends on what they say."

"That you don't indulge in it."

Gabriel shrugged. "Pleasures of the flesh are for humans." Though his mother seemed to differ on that opinion now, something that concerned him slightly. Sethios had clearly manipulated her senses somehow.

"You must be a virgin," Ezekiel said, surprising Gabriel.

"My status is neither relevant nor pertinent to our 'partnership.'" And not something Gabriel had any desire to talk about. Because he actually wasn't a virgin. He'd tried sex two years ago just to see why the humans fancied it so much, and found it quite uneventful.

Granted, it'd been with another Seraphim, who was equally curious, and they both blundered through it.

But that belied the point.

Ezekiel and Gabriel had no business discussing it, as it held no relevance whatsoever.

"Oh, it's very pertinent, but don't worry." Ezekiel clapped him on the shoulder. "I'll solve that problem for you after we handle the prophecy business."

What the hell was wrong with this being? "It's not a problem that requires solving."

"I disagree, friend. Strongly disagree."

"With what? No. Never mind. Take me to Skye so I can be finished with this business."

Ezekiel chuckled. "Unfortunately, I think we're just getting started."

Yeah, he doubted that. As soon as he had his information, he'd pass it along to Caro and head home for a long nap. Then he might venture out to procure some decent brandy. Or maybe he would try bourbon.

Ezekiel turned into a vacant alley and stopped several feet inside. "Here is good." He turned toward him, legs braced. "You mentioned entering wasn't an issue so much as locating, so I imagine you've found a way to circumvent the wards, yes?"

Gabriel folded his arms and nodded. "They are intricate, but I can weasel my way through undetected."

"Brilliant. So all you need is a location within the compound, which I have, but it will only be good for sixty minutes." Ezekiel pulled out a piece of paper with a crude drawing of what appeared to be Osiris's estate. The assassin clearly did not excel at art. "Here are the gardens at the back of the estate. This is a little pond, and beyond it is a bush maze."

"I remember seeing it." And wondering about its purpose. Seemed rather fantastical for a mansion in the middle of nowhere.

"Wandering that maze is Skye's favorite outdoor activity. Osiris grants her one hour a day outside—unaccompanied—and she always ventures there."

Interesting. "He doesn't worry that she'll use that time to try to escape?" Because Gabriel would use it to his advantage in that situation.

"No. She can't leave."

"Can't or won't?" There was a distinct difference.

"Can't."

"Because Osiris has compelled her to stay," Gabriel inferred. "There has to be a way to break it."

Ezekiel's dark eyes held his. "If you know of one, I would give you anything in return for that knowledge."

"Noted," Gabriel murmured. Ezekiel could prove useful to him, especially if he wanted to learn more about the CRF. It would be prudent to exchange information, and helping him thwart Osiris wouldn't be a hardship. "What if someone forces her to leave?" he asked, curious. "Wouldn't that make her unwilling and thereby trick the compulsion?" From what Gabriel understood, persuasion was specific, not ambiguous.

Ezekiel didn't appear fazed by the notion. If anything, his gaze glittered with memories. Bad ones.

"Osiris has compelled Skye to take her own life if she ever steps off the property, whether willingly or not." The words were uttered without emotion, but his nostrils flared at the end.

"You've tried to move her."

"Of course. Alas, no distance sways his hold over us, and his punishments are… creative."

Gabriel scratched his jaw and nodded. "Still, there has to be a way. I will look into it." If anything, because it will help him pay the debt of Ezekiel's assistance in reaching Skye.

The Ichorian neither acknowledged nor thanked him, but his stance eased ever so slightly. He couldn't afford to hope. How depressing.

"When you enter the maze, take your first two lefts. I'll meet you there, then trace you to Skye. We have a spot." The Ichorian disappeared on the final word.

"I guess that means we go now," Gabriel said to the now-empty alley. "And you'd better not be luring me into a trap."

The air crackled with laughter around him.

Gabriel didn't bother to respond to it but misted to the outskirts of Osiris's property. Fresh air and trees surrounded him a second later, forcing him to inhale deeply.

He could see the appeal to living out here. Plenty of land to roam free, perhaps even fly. Most Seraphim didn't indulge in the activity unless using it for strength training. Enjoyment was an emotion most of his kin frowned upon, but sometimes Gabriel soared through the clouds when he wanted to be alone to think. His wings stretched with the memory of his flight just last night, and his lips threatened to curl.

Already he longed to go again.

And not for practical reasons.

"Being around humans is dangerous," he muttered as he

forced himself to focus on the rune two feet before him. Only a Seraphim would spot the cleverly disguised symbol etched into a tree.

Gabriel added his own markings to temporarily deactivate the silent alarm and stepped through the barrier. Osiris might feel a slight inkling of change if he lurked nearby, but not enough to encourage investigation. More of a nuisance, like wind softly rustling the trees outside his window.

He scouted the area for the second ward and altered it in kind before fixing three more and finally stepping into the interior of the grounds.

Silence greeted his entry, confirming his success at bypassing the security measures in place. They were more a deterrent to keep out an army rather than a single individual. Osiris wouldn't fear one-off assassins, but he would want to be warned if a group of assailants had arrived. Smart magic.

Gabriel considered his surroundings before misting to the interior of the maze. He listened for any potential threats before cautiously following Ezekiel's directions. The Ichorian stood waiting for him with an impassive expression.

"Congratulations. You wasted fifteen minutes, Stark."

"Dismantling wards requires patience," he replied, unperturbed. "And this conversation will not take long."

"I'll remember that when you complain later." Ezekiel turned, his gesture obvious that he wished to be followed.

Several passages and curves later placed them near a beautiful rose garden and a gazebo filled with lilacs and other exotic flowers. A woman with raven-black hair sat waiting for them on the bench, her azure gaze expectant. She was a slight woman with pale features, but undeniably beautiful. Seraphic, even.

What is her ancestry? he wondered. Most of Osiris's abominations maintained a certain air to them that she lacked. Interesting.

Ezekiel bowed before her, his every move filled with

reverence while she watched him blankly. Gabriel expected a little more passion, perhaps even a hug, but she observed Ezekiel as one would an insect.

The relationship seemed rather one-sided.

Unrequited love, perhaps? If so, Ezekiel was far less competent than Gabriel earlier ascertained. To give up one's life over emotion was already unreasonable. To sacrifice himself for a partner who didn't share his intentions was a mark of insanity.

Skye stood, her white gown flowing to her ankles, and moved slowly toward Gabriel. "You are the faceless warrior in my visions, the one meant to help my Ezekiel free us all." She stopped right in front of him, her eyes unblinking. "You have quite a challenge before you, Seraphim. I hope you accept your path."

Riddles never intrigued him. "I'm here to learn more about my mother, not myself."

Her light blue irises held his, but he sensed she wasn't actually looking at him. "Her role differs from yours. She is the bearer of a new reign, a power unlike any this world has ever seen. Sethios will be the key to harnessing and sharpening her gifts. Without his guidance, she will destroy us all."

That didn't make any sense. "My mother possesses this skill?" Why would it manifest after a century of existence?

"Perhaps." Skye tilted her head to the side, eyes still locked on his. "The energy resides within your mother, and Sethios is the only one who can control it, but I cannot see her face clearly. It is the unknown entity that will defeat Osiris, with the aid of Sethios."

The baby, he realized. She couldn't see Caro's pregnancy but sensed the power growing *inside* of his mother. "What else can you tell me?"

Her pupils flared, giving her an eerie appeal. "You and Ezekiel will play important roles." She finally blinked, but that faraway gleam didn't leave. "Protection. Love. Freedom." Some of the haze lifted and she frowned.

"Betrayal will be required to garner favor and plant seeds. For the best rebellions grow from the ground up."

What was with seers and their obsessions with colorful phrases? "What does that mean?"

"We'll be operating on the side of evil until it's time for us to join the good," Ezekiel said. He stood several inches away from Skye, his hands clasped behind his back.

"Seven years," she rasped, her face paling. "A great sacrifice will be made by Sethios to protect her. Them. Ezekiel in the flames. Trust solidified, and faith restored." She gasped, falling to the ground on a screech that pierced the midafternoon air.

"We need to go," Ezekiel said as Skye continued to scream.

"We can't just leave her…"

"Now." Ezekiel cast a longing look at the woman convulsing on the ground before snapping his focus to the hedges. "They're coming."

The Ichorian traced without another word, leaving Gabriel no choice but to follow. He went out the way he came in, reaffirming the wards as he went, and returned to the alley they originally departed from. Finding it vacant, he wandered to the bar and sat on a stool to wait.

Ezekiel would appear. He had to. There was no way they would end their conversation on that note.

"You're back," the redheaded bartender said, grinning far too eagerly.

"Yes." He supposed that meant he needed yet another drink. "Can I try a bourbon?"

Her teeth appeared. "You can try anything you like."

Okay… "Then I'll try a bourbon," he replied slowly. "Any brand."

"I know just what you need." She winked and picked up a glass.

He sensed she meant to flirt, but he couldn't fathom why. Humans were bizarre. Ichorians, too, for that matter.

"What time do you close?" he asked, curious as to how

long he could wait here for Ezekiel. For whatever reason, this encouraged the redhead to grin widely again.

Oh. Right. She thought he wanted to know when she would be free from work.

Not quite.

"One o'clock," she murmured. "But if it's slow, I can close up early."

"One o'clock is fine," he replied, eyeing the time. That gave Ezekiel just over nine hours to appear. Should be enough time. And if he didn't, Gabriel would return tomorrow. It may require fornication with the bartender, though; otherwise, she might be a little put out by his constant visitation to her bar.

He eyed her curves as she went up onto her toes to grab a bottle from the top shelf. Long legs, too.

It could qualify as research—comparing the human experience to the Seraphim experience. The redhead was pretty enough, if a little too bubbly for his liking. Maybe he could gag her or give her mouth something else worthwhile to do.

But only if Ezekiel didn't show.

Or maybe after the Ichorian left. He did recommend Gabriel take her up as a pastime. His lower body seemed fond of the idea, especially as she leaned over the counter in a gesture meant to display her ample breasts. Why else would she wear such a low-cut top?

A brazen move.

One he should ignore but wouldn't. Gabriel never could ignore a reasonable learning opportunity.

She poured the drink in front of him. "What's your name?" she asked, hazel eyes smiling seductively.

"Stark," he replied. "Just Stark."

CHAPTER SIXTEEN

Playing House

"I'm done," Sethios called from upstairs. "Come up here when you're ready."

Caro's heart fluttered with excitement as she set the knife down on the kitchen counter. Dinner would have to wait. It would need Sethios's fine touch anyway since all her meals lacked flavor.

Seraphim prepared and ate perfectly balanced meals. If it lacked nutrients, there was no point in cooking it. Caro used to agree. Then Sethios introduced her to chocolate. He followed that up with a myriad of delicious flavors she would never forget. Now she just had to learn how to cook them.

Later.

She washed the vegetable residue from her hands and

met Sethios in the hallway outside the bedrooms.

"Show me," she demanded.

He'd spent five days in that room without allowing her entry. He claimed the paint fumes were bad for the baby, a lie they both saw right through, but she didn't press. If he wanted to surprise her, she'd allow it.

Sethios leaned against the wall, arms folded. "What do I get in return?"

"Depends on how good it is."

"As I created it all, I'd say it's near perfect."

Arrogant man. "If that's the case, then you can have whatever you want."

His lips quirked up. "You know I'm taking that as an invitation to fuck you however I want, right?"

"I hope so." Caro pressed her palm to his flat abdomen and lifted onto her toes to place a kiss against his lips. "Because that's how it was intended."

His arms slipped around her waist to hold her to him. "How impractical of you."

"On the contrary, I find it quite practical."

"Mmm." He nuzzled her nose. "I'm so glad I decided to keep you."

She smiled. "Stop delaying, Sethios. Show me what you've done."

His mouth brushed hers before he slowly shifted her in his arms. When her back met his chest, he whispered, "You're going to love it."

"Prove it."

"So eager," he murmured as he guided her forward with his hands on her hips. "I love this little demanding side of you I've unleashed."

"You give yourself too much credit." A taunt, one that excited her because she knew it would prompt Sethios to react.

"When I'm done showing you this, I'll remind you why I deserve all that credit." He nipped her neck sharply, causing her to squeal with delight.

I don't even know who I am anymore, she thought. *Why is that so thrilling?*

They stopped outside a closed door. "Go ahead, Caro. Open it," he whispered against her ear.

Her lips curved as she turned the handle, then parted as she saw what lay beyond the threshold. "Oh, Sethios…"

"One of my favorite phrases," he teased as he nudged her forward into the nursery.

"How did you do all this?" she asked, awed.

The walls were a pale blue dotted with white butterflies that reminded her of the wings she hid when in corporeal form. Stars hung from the ceiling above a crib decorated in bedding boasting similar colors, and a rocking chair sat off to the side along with a dresser and a diaper-changing table.

"You're right," she breathed before he could explain himself. "It's perfect."

"Not bad for a first-time dad, huh?" He wrapped his arms around her belly and kissed her neck. She was due in about two weeks, give or take. Sethios continued to marvel at how fast the baby grew, but Caro considered it relatively normal for a Seraphim birth.

"It's perfect," she repeated. "Is this what was in all those boxes?" The poor delivery man kept showing up with items every day, including items for other rooms in the home.

Sethios may have purchased the property, but he kept it understocked compared to the condo in Paris. She understood that he meant for this to be a last-resort location, however, so he hadn't invested as much in it. That had all changed over the last week and a half.

"Yes." He rested his chin on her shoulder. "I also ordered clothes for up to six months since I didn't know what to expect size-wise."

"She'll be small." Caro placed her hand over Sethios's forearm. "And grow the same as a human infant."

"You keep saying that, but I won't be able to believe it until I see it." He pressed a kiss to her throat and then to her cheek. "So you like it?"

"I do." Perhaps even loved it, though she didn't truly understand the difference. She fancied Sethios quite a bit as well and wondered where the lines between emotions existed.

Everything was so new to her. Seraphim simply did not live in this manner, but the more she considered it, the more she realized that all feelings held practical purposes. Happiness, for example, brightened her outlook. No longer did she see the world in black and white, but in coats of color. Whether practical or not, she preferred it.

"One more thing," he said, releasing her to retrieve a plain box from the floor. He placed it in her hands and slipped his arms around her again, chin on her shoulder. "Open it."

Caro eyed the gift with interest. "Hmm." She removed the top and peered at the shiny silver blades. "Knives."

"Knives," he confirmed softly. "To replace the ones lost in New York and Paris."

She drew her finger along the sharp edge. "You had them engraved with our initials."

"His and hers edition." He kissed her neck. "We'll keep them in the bedroom."

Her stomach tightened at the thought. "In the nightstand?"

"Naturally."

"I approve."

"I thought you might." He nipped her pulse and sighed. "Not to derail a most enlightening subject, but have you heard from Gabriel yet?"

She shook her head. Aside from the tendrils of contentment flowing from her son, she hadn't spoken to him since he dropped by their first evening in Montana.

"Are you worried about him?"

Caro shook her head again. "No. His aura is calm." She would feel his distress or pain if something nefarious had occurred.

"Will you have the same connection to our child?"

"Yes." She smiled. "I already do." Or the beginnings of it, anyway. "It's faint, but peace radiates from her when you're near." Caro determined that to be the reason why she always felt at ease in Sethios's presence, why she craved him as she did. Because he comforted Caro as well.

She set the precious box down and turned to loop her arms around his neck as he grasped her hips. "Take me to bed, please."

He smiled. "Are you addicted to me or to pleasure?"

"Both."

"Good." He kissed her all too briefly. "I need something to eat first, then I will devour you for dessert."

"What happened to demanding a reward for finishing your project?"

"Oh, I intended to collect, Caro—thoroughly—but I require sustenance first." He slid his palms to her jeans and squeezed her ass. A promise of what was to come.

"I haven't finished dinner yet, but I started it."

"Do you mind working on it while I grab a shower?"

"Only if you join me in the kitchen afterward in just a towel."

He tapped her nose with an index finger. "The student becomes the teacher." She let go of him as he bent to pick up their new fancy daggers. "I'll put these away as well."

"For later?"

He grinned, stepping backward. "I'll be down soon." Innuendo thickened his voice, his eyes flashing with intent. She would enjoy seeing what he had in mind later.

"Okay." Caro misted to the kitchen rather than taking the stairs and went about fixing dinner to the best of her ability. Chopping vegetables and grilling chicken breasts she could do. It was the seasoning bit that perplexed her. Hopefully, this combination would taste all right. She boiled some noodles, too, thinking this might be a decent Italian dish.

Sethios joined her with a towel wrapped loosely around his hips, just as she requested, and reviewed the items on the stove. "Hmm."

"Did I do it wrong?" she asked, concerned.

"Well, normally, I would add a tomato sauce or something creamier to the noodles, not butter. But we'll make this work." He retrieved some cheese from the refrigerator and a grater and started shaving pieces onto the noodles. "Stir that in until it melts."

She did as he requested while he chopped some garlic and basil behind her. Then he tossed that into the dish.

He kissed her shoulder. "Keep stirring."

Sethios grabbed the plates holding their cooked veggies and chicken from the counter and started doing something on the cutting board. When he returned, the meat was finely diced. He dropped all of it into the noodle pan, as well as some more cheese. More butter came next, followed by cream.

"I'm pretty sure you just added a thousand calories to my dish," she pointed out with a smile.

"Makeshift Alfredo." His hips pressed against her as she mixed everything together over low heat. "Your taste buds will thank me for it."

"Probably." She gave up denying it a few weeks ago. "I want chocolate for dessert."

"Sure. You can lick it off me later."

"I…" Food in the bedroom? Like warm chocolate? "I might enjoy that."

"On the contrary, darling, you'll love it." He drew his teeth along the column of her neck, and she hummed her approval just before his teeth broke the surface of her skin. His arm circled her waist to keep her against him while he indulged in her essence. The urge to return the favor and drink from him struck her hard in the chest, but she ignored the impulse.

Their relationship worked for now.

Eternity would need to be discussed later.

One day at a time.

"I think I'm addicted to you too, Caro," he whispered

after releasing her from his intoxicating bite. It always left her feeling warm and fuzzy rather than in pain and woozy. It was some sort of forbidden magic that she luxuriated in each time he drank from her.

"And to the pleasure?" she asked, referring to his comments from upstairs. *Are you addicted to me or to pleasure?*

"I've lived with pleasure for thousands of years, angel. This uncontrollable yearning started when I met you." He took the spoon from her—the one she hadn't stopped using to stir for the last several minutes—and brought it to his lips for a taste. "Gorgeous."

She shivered at the intensity in his voice. "Is it rich?"

"Very." He dipped the utensil back into the dish and brought it up to her mouth. "Open."

She did and moaned at the decadent flavor. "You're turning me into a human."

"No, I'm encouraging your inner female to come out to play." He kissed her temple and turned to pick up their plates. "Now let's eat so we can enjoy each other as dessert afterward."

Chapter Seventeen

Let's Create a Team

Eleven days.

Gabriel was on the verge of misting to Osiris's estate to find and murder Ezekiel when the Ichorian strolled through the doors of the bar with a smirk.

"I thought you might be here, mate," he greeted with a clap to Gabriel's shoulder. Ezekiel nodded at Becky—formerly known as the redheaded bartender. "I'll take one of whatever he's having."

"A scotch," she purred.

Gabriel had spent nearly the last two weeks tasting the various flavors and had found his favorite to be the brand she picked from the top shelf for Ezekiel's glass.

The assassin slid onto the stool beside him. "You two seem rather friendly."

"I had some time to kill," Gabriel replied flatly.

"So you took my advice and fucked the bartender? Nice."

He did, and they would not be discussing it. "I presume you went back to care for Skye and that's why you left me alone for the last week?" That was the only excuse he could fathom for the Ichorian pulling the disappearing act. Skye's screech still buzzed in his ears. Gabriel had never heard anything like it.

"Yes." Ezekiel accepted the drink from Becky and smiled. "Thanks, love. Can you give us a few minutes to chat privately?"

Her hazel eyes locked on Gabriel, and he nodded his agreement. Just because she'd seen him naked—several times—didn't mean she had the right to know his business. She must have seen the resolve in his gaze because she huffed and slunk off to the other side of the bar.

"Your bedside manner could use some serious help," Ezekiel remarked casually.

Gabriel ignored him. "What happened to Skye?"

"She had a vision—a violent one."

"Regarding Caro's child?" He assumed Ezekiel knew by now about the baby, especially after Skye's comments pertaining to the energy inside Caro.

"Regarding us all." The assassin took a long sip of his drink, finishing nearly all of it before setting it down. "Skye has perfected the art of reiterating her visions to Osiris in a rather cryptic manner. He believes she witnessed the downfall of his enemies, which would be the unknown entity and Sethios. As such, he's quite pleased at present. What he doesn't know is that you and I will be responsible for that downfall."

Gabriel swirled the contents of his glass. "I hope you have more details than that." Because no way would he ever betray his mother.

"Oh, I have more than details. I have a full-fledged plan. And you, my Seraphim friend, are going to help whether you approve or not." He finished his drink and stood. "Let's go. There's someone I need you to meet."

Golden flecks swirled vivaciously through the Ichorian's black irises, glinting with promise and excitement. Whatever he had in mind clearly energized him.

"Tell me the plan."

"On the way," Ezekiel replied. "We're losing time."

"Oh, so now you're in a hurry?" Gabriel asked.

"I'll bring you back to your precious bartender for more playtime later. I promise."

Gabriel didn't even blink. "That's not what I meant to imply."

"I know." Ezekiel's grin was devilish in nature and so very appropriate. "Either follow me or don't. But you will be helping whether you like it or not." He tossed a large bill beside his empty glass and turned toward the exit without a backward glance.

Well. Gabriel could choose not to play this game and wait for his supposed involvement, or he could follow the Ichorian.

Right.

He'd sat here long enough waiting. Might as well see what the assassin had in mind.

Gabriel added to the funds on the bar top and started after the Ichorian.

"Stark!" Becky called as he reached the door.

He turned with an eyebrow arched, and she gave him an exasperated look. "Yes?" he asked.

"Ugh, never mind," she huffed, her hands on her hips.

What did she expect? A kiss goodbye? Promises of tomorrow?

He snorted. *Not going to happen*. He didn't bother to wave before joining a smirking Ezekiel on the sidewalk. The Ichorian shook his head slowly and laughed. "We'll have to work on that, mate."

"On what?"

Ezekiel started walking. "Your manners."

"My manners are fine," he replied as he strolled along beside him.

"Not by human standards."

"I'm not human."

"Clearly." Ezekiel turned in to the same alley they departed from before and held out his hand. "You'll need my assistance this time."

"How does your ability work?" Gabriel wondered, neither accepting nor denying his request. "You track by blood and then mist there?"

"I essentially wrap myself in shadows and move with them to wherever the essence I desire exists. It doesn't necessarily need to be blood, though that is how I track breathing beings. I can also trace to a location of my choosing, similar to teleporting, if someone I'm tracking is nearby. That's how I located you that first day near the CRF."

Similar to Araceli's line of tracking genes. All the Ichorians and Hydraians possessed gifts similar to the various Seraphim families. Gabriel didn't quite follow the genetics, but it was clear that Osiris's gift of life altered the human genome upon rebirth and triggered hidden talents.

Gabriel reached for Ezekiel's hand. "Let's go."

"Brilliant."

Blackness swarmed Gabriel's vision for a few seconds, then disappeared to reveal a balcony overlooking a black sand beach. A white-walled home with a bright blue roof sat off to the right, a pool rested below, and a hill dotted with similarly styled houses stood on the left. "We're in Hydria," he realized, recognizing the Greek architecture "Why?"

"Me," a voice said softly behind him.

Gabriel turned to find a dark-skinned man standing awkwardly inside, his posture rigid. His dark gaze lifted to Ezekiel, uncertainty radiating from him.

"Owen," the Ichorian greeted with a grin. "You really need to loosen up. If I wanted you dead, you would be."

"You're notorious for playing with your victims before

slaughtering them," the young Hydraian pointed out. "Forgive me for not trusting you."

Ezekiel collapsed into an oversized sofa just inside and sighed. "My reputation is old and matured. Besides, I'm no longer bored. Not with my new purposes, anyway."

Gabriel leaned his shoulder against the door frame and folded his arms. "Start explaining, Ezekiel. I'm done waiting."

Owen gaped at him, his expression clearly stating his fear of retaliation from the assassin on the couch. He clearly had poor survival instinct since Gabriel was the more lethal of the two.

"Owen, this is Stark," Ezekiel said, introducing them. "He's a Seraphim."

The poor kid almost fell as he hurriedly backed away from Gabriel. "The fuck is he doing here?" he asked, his voice quivering.

"He's part of the plan." Ezekiel sounded far too cheerful.

"And what is the plan?" Gabriel demanded.

The Ichorian grinned. "We're going to take down Osiris."

CHAPTER EIGHTEEN

Picking the Right Path

Caro couldn't see her feet. In one week, her belly had gone from somewhat showing to fully enlarged.

"Wow," Sethios breathed from the doorway. He'd just been out for a run, something she could definitely not do in her current condition.

Sweat glistened on his flat abdomen, giving Caro the urge to go onto her knees and lick him clean. Except that would really hurt her back and she'd probably end up on her butt. He seemed oblivious to her plight as he sauntered forward and placed his palm on her stomach.

"You look ready to pop, Caro."

"I feel ready to pop," she admitted. "Our daughter has been doing somersaults inside me all morning, and I'm very ready for her to stop." As she spoke, the little being did another kick.

Sethios's eyes grew wide, and he dropped to his knees. "I felt that."

"Me too." Caro winced as their daughter repeated the action. "Gabriel rarely moved like this."

"No, he probably just sat there and waited for you to tell him to come out. He seems like the type who enjoys being bored, anyway." Sethios lifted her oversized dress—one he had ordered online especially for her—and placed a kiss above her belly button. This was meant not to seduce but to cherish.

Caro fell a little harder for him in that moment. Gabriel's father never once visited her while she carried their child, nor did he bother to check on her or his son after the birth. Not that she expected him to—it wasn't the Seraphim way.

Having this new experience to compare to, however, she found she preferred Sethios's methods more. His presence calmed her, to the point that she was hardly sick. A significant improvement from her first experience.

"Hi, little one," he whispered.

"Oh," Caro moaned as their child reacted to her father's voice and touch. "I think she likes you."

"Of course she does," Sethios murmured, his finger reverently stroking her stomach. "I convinced her mother to indulge in chocolate and other more gratifying activities." He waggled his brows up at her while she rolled her eyes.

"Somehow I doubt she'll be all that enthused by the latter."

"It's what created her." He fixed her dress as he stood and slid his palm to her lower back. "It pleases her mother too." His lips whispered over hers. "And it convinced her mother to feel."

She grinned against his mouth. "I still don't think she'll want all the details."

"Certainly not," he agreed softly. "How are you feeling, love?"

"Heavy, hungry, and hot."

"Alliteration, hmm?" He chuckled. "Give me five minutes to shower, and I'll fix you something to eat." He kissed her far too gently and wandered off, losing his shorts and socks in the process.

She leaned against their shared bed. Misting to the kitchen would take a lot out of her, and she needed her strength. If Osiris found them now, it would be hard enough to mist herself and the baby out, and she refused to leave Sethios behind.

Blood bond, her soul whispered.

The urge intensified every day, but she continued to repress it. The chances Sethios would agree to an eternal bond were slim anyway. He might be besotted with her now, but they'd barely known each other two months. That was a blip in time for two immortals. He also mentioned not being the monogamous type. They agreed on here and now; the future would be determined as they went.

Caro's soul might be on board with keeping him forever, but her heart and mind remained unconvinced.

Liar, her soul chastised.

"Enough," she muttered, pushing off the bed and right into Gabriel's appearing form. She bounced right back into the mattress with a grunt and shook her head. "Ow." Her body throbbed from the unexpected impact as her heart kick-started in alarm. "I didn't sense you."

"I didn't give a warning," Gabriel murmured. "Sorry. I finally have all the information I need and returned as quickly as possible."

"Still haven't learned to knock, I see," Sethios commented as he wandered in with a towel slung loosely around his hips. Water trickled down from his hair to his shoulders, shimmering in the low light of their bedroom. Again the urge to lick water from his abs hit her in the gut— something he knew, because he winked at her.

Arrogant man.

"Have you made all the arrangements to stay here?" Gabriel asked, ignoring Sethios.

"For now, yes," Caro replied, rubbing her belly. She wasn't exactly sitting on the bed so much as leaning heavily against it. "Sethios assembled the nursery and ordered everything we need for an infant, including several additional items. We haven't planned for the long term, though."

"Start planning," Gabriel replied. "At least seven years."

"Seven years?" Sethios pulled a maroon shirt over his head and joined them. "That's rather specific."

"Skye had another prophecy."

"Another one," Sethios mused. "Great. Do we have all the details on the first yet?" He settled beside Caro and wrapped an arm around her lower back, offering support right where she needed it.

How does he always seem to know?

"Yes," Gabriel replied. "But it's so much greater than that. The prophecy isn't about you or Caro so much as your child. According to Skye, your progeny will have the strength and will to destroy Osiris and his bloodline."

The words sat heavily between them as Caro dissected their meaning. "His bloodline," she repeated slowly. "As in Ichorians and Hydraians."

"Yes." Gabriel locked gazes with Sethios. "Unless you convince the child otherwise."

Sethios's eyebrows rose. "You mean, use my gift for persuasion to tell her not to?"

"Her?" Gabriel glanced at Caro and she nodded, confirming the gender. She was certain they were having a girl. Motherly intuition and all that. Gabriel's gaze brightened infinitesimally before he refocused on Sethios's question.

"No. Your humanity is what will ground her and potentially alter her destiny." He held up his hand to indicate he wasn't done explaining. "Osiris has created a problem, and she is the solution, thereby making her the perfect weapon. That's why the Seraphim want Caro to return and raise her among our kind. They wish to craft her logical frame of mind and use her to fulfill one potential future path."

"What's the other potential?" Caro asked, knowing various alternatives always existed. That's why the seers played this game; they enjoyed altering the future to meet their needs.

"Osiris's demise is prevalent in all potential outcomes, but the destruction of Ichorians and Hydraians only exists in one thus far. The one where you raise her among our kind, without Sethios's influence."

"I see," Sethios replied, his arm leaving her back as he stood. "And which path do you prefer, Gabriel?"

Tension radiated between the two males, causing Caro to frown. "It's not up to him," she murmured. "We will decide her fate."

"No." Sethios took a step toward her son. "He's already chosen. I can see it in his eyes. The question is, which path? Because we both know the only way Caro will raise *our* child without me is if I'm not in the picture. So what did you decide, Gabriel?"

Her son met Sethios's gaze without flinching. "Skye's second prophecy involves a betrayal of the worst kind, one that ends badly for both of you. And you both will suffer. Horribly."

"Meaning you've chosen path one to save Caro and dispense of me, as well as all of Osiris's bloodline."

"It is the logical choice," Gabriel replied, his green eyes intensifying. "Alas, no. That is not what I have chosen."

Caro's brow crinkled in confusion as Sethios asked, "Why?"

"While it is the logical recourse with the most desired of outcomes, it will hurt my mother." His gaze shifted to Caro. "At one point, you would have agreed with this path to destroy Osiris and his abominations. I sense that has changed. Am I wrong?"

Both males studied her intently, causing her stomach to churn uncomfortably.

Did she want to destroy Osiris? Absolutely. No question.

Did she want to destroy his abominations? Her lips flattened. Two months ago, it wouldn't have been a thought. They shouldn't exist. Osiris created them to spite the High Council of Seraph, and perhaps because he was bored. Or worse, to use as an army.

She met Sethios's green eyes, his expression sheltered while she considered his fate and those, presumably, of his friends. He didn't choose to be an abomination. Osiris did. To punish him for his father's crimes seemed... wrong.

Further, to force her child to be the one to deliver that punishment to Osiris and his bloodline didn't feel right.

It was her child's destiny, according to the seers, just as it was Caro's destiny to sleep with Sethios and produce their daughter. Someone should have warned Caro of her destiny and given her the choice to see it through. And that, truly, wasn't all that much of a life-changing decision. Raising a child took time and care, and eighteen years wasn't long for someone who lived for eternity.

Destroying a higher being and his entire bloodline, however, was a much bigger task and responsibility. One that could cost their daughter her life, or worse, her soul. The seers and Seraphim wouldn't be bothered by that risk if it meant destroying Osiris. They would sacrifice several souls if that's what it took to accomplish the task. Just as they had given away Caro's body without blinking an eye.

Yet they couldn't be bothered to handle Osiris before this.

So why now? Why *her* daughter? Because they couldn't do it without her, or some other reason?

Everything the Seraphim did, specifically the seers, served some purpose. But who actually decided which purpose to pursue and which to ignore? The High Council? The seers?

Seraphim, by nature, were not meant to be biased. Yet, Caro couldn't help feeling a bit of uncertainty after having been sent here under false pretenses to birth a child—something she may have agreed to willingly had they only asked.

And that was the point. They never did.

"She deserves a choice," she said finally. "It's not about what I want or believe but about her choice. If she's raised with the Seraphim, she'll never be allowed to decide for herself." Her daughter must have agreed with her words because she chose that moment to shift again, this time in a somewhat painful somersault that expelled the air from Caro's lungs.

Easy, please, she whispered. *This is important.*

"How would you feel if our daughter destroyed my father *and* his bloodline?" Sethios asked, his patient tone belied by the fire brewing in his alluring gaze.

"I… I don't know," she admitted.

"You don't know," he repeated slowly. "You would be okay with her committing a massacre and annihilating an entire population of beings?"

"They were never meant to be," Caro said through her gritted teeth. Her abdomen felt abnormally tight. She tried to lean more against the bed, but it didn't help loosen her at all. At Sethios's cocked brow, she added, "Osiris created them against the natural order."

"He created me against the natural order as well, Caro," he pointed out. "Making me, what, good enough to fuck and nothing else?" He shook his head sadly, taking another step away from her. "And here I thought we were getting somewhere."

"It's not… that's not…" God, her stomach hurt. A lot. She held her lower belly as she tried to form the words Sethios needed, but her mind kept splintering with the pain slicing up from her center. "I don't know any—" She exhaled sharply, her words cutting off before she could finish.

"And because you have not met any, aside from myself and Ezekiel, that makes it okay to exterminate an entire race of immortals? Two, technically, if you consider Hydraians separate from Ichorians."

She swallowed roughly. "Ezekiel wanted to kill me when we first met." Not that she could hold that against the entire race. Her daughter shifted to Caro's bladder, making it impossible to add more to that statement as she fought her body's innate reaction to that move.

And now I'm slightly wet down there and not in the way I would prefer.

She blinked.

What a completely inappropriate thought.

"Because he thought you were human," Sethios growled. "So that justifies your hatred of all Ichorians? Ezekiel is a dick and not the best representation."

"And you are?" she asked, meaning to tease and realizing too late that it had the opposite impact.

His green eyes smoldered with fury. "Destroying Osiris, I understand. Fuck, I want to kill him myself. But his bloodline? It would include her need to kill me, her father. Do you want that on her conscience? Can you live with that on your own conscience?" Quiet questions filled with deep-seated emotions she couldn't name.

Pain ricocheted up her spine, forcing her to close her eyes. Her tongue hurt from biting it so hard. He wanted an answer, but she couldn't voice it. Not without screaming.

"I see," he murmured. "Good to know where we stand."

"Can I interrupt?" Gabriel asked, his voice bored.

"Is this the part where you try to remove me from the picture so I won't interfere with the Seraphim plans for my child? Because I think you'll be in for quite the surprise." Sethios sounded flippant, almost to the point of cruel. And from the trajectory of his voice, he stood on the opposite side of the room, near the door.

"No," Gabriel replied. "This is the part where I suggest we help Caro, as she's going into labor."

Her eyes flashed open to meet his light green eyes, then widened at the realization that he was correct. "She's early."

Gabriel shrugged. "Only by a few days. I'll go grab some towels."

Sethios was at her side in the next instant, his touch gentle as he helped her onto the mattress.

"Oh, you don't want—"

"I'll replace it," he replied, following her statement about ruining the bed without her having to finish it. "Just lie down."

She did as he suggested and winced at the jabbing pain in her side. Still, she had to say something… "Sethios?"

"Yes?" Despite being near, his soft tone lacked the warmth she'd become accustomed to. As did his green eyes as she met his gaze. The note of concern was nice, but she wanted the other emotion he displayed, the one that helped her feel… cherished.

"I couldn't—" She cut off on a cry as agony ripped through her stomach. "Something's… wrong." She exhaled the words but couldn't inhale to replenish the oxygen.

"Caro?" His brow came down, then lifted at whatever he saw in her face. "Caro!"

She tried to respond but couldn't. Her throat felt tight. Her lungs too. Everything refused to work, as if frozen in time.

Everything except her heart.

It beat frantically as she fought to breathe but couldn't. Then shattered at the anguished expression pulling at Sethios's features.

"Don't do this to me, angel. Come on. Breathe." Warmth caressed her cheeks and neck, but it faltered beneath everything else.

And then she was floating. High in the clouds. No. Too light. Maybe. She blinked back into the room, then back to the clouds, and then back again.

A familiar presence surrounded her. Sethios holding her? Calling her name? She couldn't be sure. Everything drifted in and out, in and out…

This couldn't be happening, not now. There was still so

much for her to say.

Her thoughts about the blood bond.

Her thoughts about *him*.

About their future.

About the future of their child.

She wouldn't choose one of destruction. And while, yes, she thought the abomination problem needed to be handled, it was more about Osiris than anything else.

Sethios isn't an abomination.

Or maybe he was.

Either way, she still adored him. Maybe even loved him, if that emotion existed for Seraphim.

Blackness swarmed her vision, taking over the clouds and the room all at once.

Save her, she prayed. *Save our daughter.*

CHAPTER NINETEEN

A New Power Rises

"Move," Gabriel ordered.

"Fuck off," Sethios growled as his hands ran over Caro's lifeless form on the bed. She'd lost consciousness, something he intended to fix. Somehow. Maybe.

Fuck!

"Have you ever delivered a Seraphim child? No. So move. Now." Gabriel shoved him out of the way. Behind him stood a gorgeous woman with blonde hair, porcelain skin, and blue-green eyes.

"Where the fuck did you come from?" Sethios snapped, his attention torn between the newcomer and killing Caro's son.

"No time." Gabriel moved to the side. "Help her, Leela."

The woman stepped forward with a bag and started pulling out supplies. "I need warm water," she advised. "And more towels."

Gabriel misted while Sethios eyed the female. "You're a Seraphim."

"Yes," she replied.

He didn't have the energy to ask more, nor did he care so long as she helped Caro and the baby.

He swept his palm over his face and sighed. *Shit.* He'd been so frustrated with Caro's words that he'd failed to notice her deteriorating condition, and rather than be there for her, he had pushed her away.

I'm a bastard.

Sethios knelt beside Caro and clasped her ice-cold hand between his.

"Come on, sweetheart," he whispered. "Don't do this to me. Come back." Her pale face and purple lips broke his heart.

If anything happens to her… He didn't know how to finish that thought. She would survive. She had to.

"She'll be fine," Gabriel said as he reappeared. "Most females die a few times during birth due to the intensity of the process. It takes a lot of energy to birth a Seraphim, especially one as powerful as my future sister."

"What can I do?" Sethios asked, helpless.

Gabriel blinked at him. "Provide comfort. It may… help."

"That doesn't sound very scientific," Sethios pointed out even as he leaned in to press a kiss to Caro's forehead.

"It's not, but my mother's pregnancy responded well to your brand of care; therefore, the birthing process might be the same. Only time will tell."

"She's only dilated three inches," Leela murmured. "There's not enough time."

"Time for what? The baby to be delivered normally?" Sethios demanded. "We can't wait?"

"It's not a matter of us waiting, but the child," Gabriel

replied. "Seraphim heal from any injury, including a breach such as this."

Sethios shuddered at the implication of what he meant and slid into the bed beside Caro to hold her as best he could.

He brushed his lips against her temple, then her cheek, and willed her to return to him so they could do this together. All the hurt her words caused evaporated as he focused on their child and keeping Caro safe.

He palmed her belly and whispered, "Not yet, little one. Give your mom a bit to acclimate. Please." The last thing he wanted to see was Caro being ripped open by their child.

"It won't help," Leela said, her voice oddly emotional for a Seraphim. "As Gabe said, the babe will come whether Caro's body is ready or not."

"I warned you this pregnancy hasn't been normal." Gabriel eyed Sethios's hand on Caro's belly. "The baby responds to him."

Sethios ignored them and focused on his future daughter. "Wait for your mom, sweetheart. Please. I know you don't want to hurt her." He stroked Caro's stomach while speaking and kept his mouth near her ear. Leela and Gabriel likely thought him insane, and maybe he was, but he had to try something. He couldn't just lie there while Caro suffered.

So much had changed these last two months. What started as a fun pastime blossomed into something he never could have imagined wanting—a family.

Sethios wasn't meant to be a dad. He certainly had no desire to be one. Nor did he want a monogamous relationship with a child's mother.

But Caro... She altered everything, including his perspective on life.

He *enjoyed* playing house with her. Perhaps because it was so new, or maybe because of some deeper connection he refused to acknowledge.

Regardless of the cause, his eyes had been opened to a

new possibility of how to live. One where he truly possessed a purpose—to nurture and grow a little one. To adore and cherish a person other than himself.

Caro's fingers twitched in his hand as the baby kicked his opposite palm. Her eyes remained closed, but her pulse kicked up a notch.

"Caro?" he whispered.

"Sethios," she breathed.

He hadn't known what to expect, but hearing his name on her tongue, even as soft and painful as it was, sent a jolt of electricity right to his heart.

Thank fuck for immortality.

"I'm right here," he assured her. "You're okay, love."

"Don't—" She broke off on a harsh cough, her body convulsing with the movement.

"Shh, don't try to speak." He drew soothing circles over her belly. "Both of you need to relax."

She shook her head, her eyes still closed. "No. I don't want…" She swallowed, her throat constricting on the words.

"Don't want what, angel?" he asked, concerned. *She had better not say she doesn't want me.* He'd been an ass before, but she'd essentially said she didn't care if he died. And worse, she didn't care if their own child killed him.

"You're an abomination." Her fingers curling into a fist inside his palm as his heart stopped beating. Was she really going to continue this conversation now? In the middle of giving birth? Did the woman have a death wish?

"But," she continued, her voice hoarse. She cleared her throat twice before proceeding while his entire body lay frozen beside hers. "But you're *my* abomination."

He frowned, not following. "We can discuss this after—"

"No," she said, a little stronger, her eyes opening finally to reveal two pools of liquid sapphire. "You're *my* abomination, Sethios. *Mine.*" She unfurled her fist to press her palm to his. "No one may kill you. No one."

He blinked, surprised.

When he'd asked earlier if she could stomach their own child killing him, she hadn't responded. He had assumed it was because she didn't know. But the vehemence in her gaze now suggested she more than knew where she stood on the subject. She didn't reply originally because she couldn't.

Now, even while their daughter was essentially ripping her insides apart, the first thing she fought to do was not to give birth but to tell him how she felt.

Mine.

He swallowed under the emotion that single word instilled inside of him. Because he felt that way about her too. Not that he wanted to admit it out loud. Especially with their current audience.

They still needed to discuss her outlook on Ichorians and Hydraians, as well as their daughter's apparent future, but that could be handled over time.

"Did you just profess your love to me, angel?" He pitched his voice low in an attempt to tease her and diffuse the intense atmosphere in the room, but her lips didn't twitch.

"Yes." No hesitation or light-headedness in her tone. Not even a blink.

"Oh, Caro." He cradled her face between his palms. "You're emotional right now. We'll talk about all of this after the baby is born, okay?"

"I mean it, Sethios," she said, utter conviction underlining her words. "I would never condone—" She cried out in pain, ending whatever else she wanted to say.

Sethios immediately returned his hand to her stomach. "Stop, little one. You're hurting your mom." Urgency and demand filled his voice while Caro shuddered beside him. He slid his other palm from her face to the back of her neck as she tilted her head into his shoulder. "Shh, love, it's okay."

"Please don't let go," she whispered. "Please."

"Never, angel." He kissed the top of her head. "I'll never

let go." The words escaped him as if pulled from his soul. Never had he promised a woman forever, or even tomorrow, but he expelled the statement so easily for Caro. And he found, shockingly, that he meant it.

Could this be love? Did a being of his history have that potential? He certainly didn't deserve to have her care and devotion, nor should she truly desire his in return, but he wouldn't curse fate for this gift.

Sethios refused to overthink it. He would live in the moment and enjoy the sensations while they lasted. Because tomorrow, everything could change.

"Fascinating," Leela mused, reminding him of her presence. "You were right, Gabe. The babe is reacting to his command."

Gabriel stood leaning against the wall on the opposite side of the room, his arms folded and his expression bored. He lifted one shoulder in response. Nothing more.

"You didn't finish telling us about the prophecy." Because Sethios had derailed the conversation and demanded to know which path the Seraphim intended to walk down.

"It's already started," Gabriel replied. "My mother wishes to give my sister a choice in her fate. It's a decision driven by emotion, but I understand it and also happen to agree. Which means I'll be working with Ezekiel far more than I would like in the near future."

"Ezekiel?" Sethios repeated. "Why?"

"Our destinies are intertwined" was all he said.

Sethios would have requested more details, but the movement in Caro's stomach required his focus. "Stay calm," he whispered to the baby. "We're all going to do this together."

"I can sense her love for you through the bond." Awe lit up Caro's expression, her eyes glittering with warmth. "She trusts you."

"This proves what I've been saying," Leela said conversationally. "Not that the council will listen to me. I'm too emotional for them." The female rolled her eyes in a very non-Seraphim-like manner.

"She's from the fertility line," Caro explained, catching his thoughts.

Leela snorted. "That's a fancy term for lust. I specialize in sex, which apparently qualifies me to be a midwife."

Two months ago, the very beautiful woman would have intrigued him. But another Seraphim had captured his eye and tamed him in a way he never thought possible.

Caro was the only one he wanted.

Still, he had to ask, "You specialize in sex, in what capacity?"

"Wouldn't you like to know," the female replied, grinning wickedly.

Caro's hand slipped to Sethios's wrist where she dug her nails into his skin. He leaned in to kiss her before she could utter a complaint and rubbed his nose against hers.

"You're mine too, love," he whispered. "I was only curious."

Her blue eyes burned into his. "Good."

He smiled. "I rather like this possessive side to you. We'll have to explore it more later."

"Much later," Leela cut in. "Because the baby is ready, as is Caro."

Sethios's neck twisted so fast that it was a wonder his head didn't fall off. "Now?"

"Yes," Caro and Leela said at the same time.

He gave up trying to understand the baby process. Everything he thought he knew didn't apply. Two-month gestational period. Less-than-an-hour labor period. Dying immortals who miraculously healed. Babies who heeded his command.

Sure. Why not?

"Do I need to do anything?" he asked, voice remarkably calm given the situation.

Caro squeezed his hand. "Talk to her. She likes your voice."

Also bizarre, but his daughter apparently would possess the power to destroy an entire bloodline. Why should this shock him?

He kissed Caro once more before drawing patterns over her exposed belly and cooing, "Okay, little one. It's time, but be nice to your mom, okay? She has a death grip on my hand, and I don't want to lose it."

Caro responded by tightening her hold on him, something that would have concerned him more if she hadn't also giggled with the move.

There's my angel, he thought warmly.

Her pain tolerance had to be high given everything her body had experienced these last two months. The sweat dotting her brow and the stress lines around her mouth were the only indications that whatever was happening hurt.

He continued to lightly trace her stomach and speak to their daughter. "I can't wait to meet you, sweetheart," he admitted softly. "I hope you resemble your mom more than me, though. She's far prettier."

"Liar," Caro breathed, her eyes closed as she focused on expelling a living being from her body.

Holy fuck, this is happening.

I'm going to be a dad.

He knew that already. But the reality crashed into him as Leela told Caro to give her first push. Nothing happened, but he sensed their child was on the verge of entering the world.

"She's stubborn," Caro grumbled. "*That* would be from her father's side."

Sethios chuckled even as he beamed at the possibility. "Pretty sure that's a combined effort, darling."

"Another push now," Leela urged. "Come on, Caro."

An ache shot up his arm as his angel grasped his hand in earnest. Not to punish, but for support, and he gave it to her. Fuck, she was bringing a miracle into the world. A few broken bones hardly compared.

"She's crowning," Leela announced.

"I know!" Caro growled, her brow dripping sweat. "Fuck!"

Sethios bit his lip to keep from chuckling at what appeared to be her new favorite word. She used it around him fairly often, usually when she wanted something from him.

"Come on, Caro. I know you've got more in you than this," Leela chastised. "Keep going."

An unfavorable reply fell from Caro's lips, causing Leela to chuckle. Definitely not a normal Seraphim. Where did Gabriel find her? He glanced at the stoic male still leaning casually against the wall. No way were these two lovers. Friends, maybe. If the guy even had any of those.

Another pang screamed up his forearm as his angel borrowed strength from him.

"You're doing great, love," he murmured, having no idea whether or not that was true.

Her expression was that of a warrior goddess, all fire and fight, highlighted by glorious blonde waves of hair and a face blessed by the heavens. Finding her alluring in that moment probably went against the grain, but Sethios doubted he would ever find her unattractive.

"Wow," Leela said, awed by whatever she saw between Caro's legs. An inappropriate reply stalled in his mouth when he *felt* his daughter's presence. Similar to how he sensed his father's arrival, but far more powerful.

"Why isn't she crying?" he asked, awed.

"She's content." Caro's whisper-soft reply drew his attention to her pale cheeks and discolored eyes. Her irises held an eerie white glow that did not appear natural in the slightest.

"Caro," he slid closer to her on the bed, both of his hands going to her face. "Talk to me, sweetheart."

"Is… fine," she slurred, her eyes rolling back in her head. She began to convulse as magic sifted in the air, and she blinked between her ethereal state and corporeal state, over and over.

"Leela, tell me this is normal," he demanded.

"It's normal," she replied automatically.

He cursed, realizing he'd forced that reply on accident. "Tell me what's happening."

"Power exchange," Gabriel replied calmly. "Which is normal. She's bonding with your daughter."

Caro didn't let go of his hand, nor did her grip lessen, but that didn't keep him from worrying. He watched as her essence shifted, colors flashing in navy and azure hues as her wings appeared and disappeared, and her eyes blinked rapidly.

"See," Leela whispered.

It took effort to remove his gaze long enough to see what she held, and then his jaw hit the floor. His daughter was bundled and already clean. "How… ?"

"You were too focused on Caro to notice," Leela murmured. "And your daughter didn't cry."

"Is that common?" he asked, concerned. Most babies were supposed to cry, right?

"For a Seraphim, yes." Another comment from Gabriel.

"She's bathing in her mother's aura." Leela smiled down at the tiny child in her arms. She'd swaddled her in a towel, hiding everything except her face.

"She looks just like Caro." His voice broke on the words as a warmth unlike any he'd ever felt caressed his chest. "She's absolutely perfect."

He kept one palm pressed to Caro's cheek while he reached out to brush his knuckles against his daughter's face. Electricity hummed through him at the touch, escalating his heartbeat.

"So much power," Leela marveled. "I've been doing this for centuries, and I've never felt anything like it." Her blue-green irises lifted to Gabriel. "What have you pulled me into?"

"The future," the Seraphim replied. "Everything is going to change."

Her lips curled into a devious grin. "About damn time."

CHAPTER TWENTY

Eternity Redefined

Sethios played with a lock of Caro's hair while she slept. He'd bathed her—something Leela recommended—and when he returned, the mattress and bedding maintained no signs of what had taken place just an hour prior. The only proof lay asleep in the bassinet beside the bed.

His daughter.

None of it matched what he expected, but he gave up asking questions. Seraphim were very clearly not human.

Caro yawned as she snuggled into his chest, her body already healing to its natural form. Another immortal quality. No one would be able to tell that she'd just given birth, let alone been pregnant at all.

"Fascinating," he whispered, awed by the entire experience.

His daughter responded with a small sound of contentment beside him. He lifted onto an elbow to peer down into the bassinet and found her gazing up at him with bright green eyes that resembled his own. So much for Caro's theory about newborn Seraphim resembling human babies.

"From what I understand, you should have blue eyes," he told her. "But they are definitely my shade of green." And radiating an intelligence that bespoke of her supernatural heritage.

"Let me see her," Caro said softly. "Please."

He switched focus to the gorgeous blonde curled against his side. "You were asleep."

"I felt her wake, and your words confirmed it." She stretched, causing the sheet to lower over her breasts. Any other time and he would have taken that as an invitation. But they had an audience.

He sat up and studied his daughter.

"Hi, sweetheart," he cooed. "Want to see your mom?"

God, she was small. She could easily fit in the palm of his hand, something he realized as he gently lifted her. He didn't know much about babies, but instinct had him cradling her head and gingerly moving her into the crook of his arm.

"Oh," Caro breathed as he rotated toward her. "She's perfect."

"Just like her mom." He brushed his knuckles over their daughter's cheek and smiled. "You need a name, little angel."

"Do you have one in mind?" Caro asked, her bright gaze on the child in his arms.

He considered and nodded. "I do."

"Share." A demand, not a request.

His lips curled at the impatience in her tone. Already his Caro was back to the angel he adored.

"*Anastasia* means 'resurrection' in ancient Greek, but it's far too plain for her." He brushed his knuckles down her neck to the blanket cocooning her tiny form. So soft. "How do you feel about Astasiya?" He didn't ask Caro, but his daughter. "A variation of Anastasia, but unique and empowering, and beautiful."

Delight tugged at his heart, confirming his choice.

"She approves," Caro murmured. "As do I. We can call her Stas for short."

"That's a popular male human name in Russia and Eastern Europe," Gabriel informed from the doorway. "But suitable."

Sethios glanced up to see Leela beaming beside Gabriel, her gaze on the baby. *Definitely not a normal Seraphim.*

"She's a future heartbreaker," the blonde declared, her mirth apparent. "I look forward to knowing her in a few decades." She glanced at her wrist as if checking the time, but she didn't wear a watch. "Well, I do believe my work here is done. Unless you all require me for anything else?"

"A rune," Gabriel said.

All eyes were immediately trained on him, but it was Caro who spoke first. "Excuse me?"

"Astasiya requires something subtle, a marking that disguises her as a fledgling. Something to explain her immunity to Ichorian gifts and to make her vulnerable to Hydraians, at least until her coming of age."

"Why would we do that?" Sethios demanded. An invisible grip constricted his heart, reminding him of the vulnerable being cradled against his chest. "Sorry, little angel." Whether it was the word or tone she didn't care for, he didn't know. "You're very wrong about this resembling a regular human birth, Caro." Because he was certain newborns didn't react in this manner.

"She's far from average, even for a Seraphim." Pride colored her tone even as she narrowed her gaze at Gabriel. For being covered only by a sheet, she appeared quite regal. "Explain the need for the rune."

"It's for her protection." He finally stepped into the room, but merely to lean back against the wall with his hands in his jean pockets. "According to Skye, she will one day be mistaken as a fledgling and the rune will explain away some of her abnormalities. It will essentially protect her identity until such a time that she is ready for the world to truly know her."

Sethios snorted at the reasoning. "We'll be here to protect her, thereby making that additional requirement moot."

"No. You won't." For the first time, emotion flickered in the Seraphim's gaze. It was brief, but deep, and radiated a sadness that silenced the room. "Skye has altered the prophecies in such a way that Osiris is unaware of Astasiya. But in seven years, a sacrifice will be required to protect her identity. If either of you refuses, he will learn of her, and she will be destroyed."

The air around them chilled with his words, freezing Sethios's heart. He couldn't speak and neither, apparently, could Caro.

"Ezekiel created a plan that I perfected, but it involves several chess moves that have to line up to work. One misstep and we risk Astasiya." He locked gazes with Caro. "I have heard all the possible scenarios, Mother, and while the easier path would be to raise and protect Astasiya among Seraphim, I remain unconvinced that she will be safe there. This, in my informed opinion, is the best path, and I am prepared to take a blood oath. For my sister."

Caro and Leela gasped, causing Sethios's eyebrows to inch downward. "What does that mean?" he asked.

"He's offering to pledge fealty to Astasiya," Caro explained, her voice filled with wonder. "It's an honor only bestowed upon members of the High Council."

"If the prophecies are right, which, I believe, they are, then the members of the High Council no longer warrant my loyalty. My sister, however, does. And she will require my guidance to succeed in your absence. This is the only way."

"By committing to her, he will be outlawed from the

Seraphim community and thereby free to do as he pleases among humans. Which would grant him the flexibility to watch over her as needed." Caro shook her head sadly. "I cannot ask that of you, Gabriel. You've already done enough."

"You're not asking me to do anything. I'm telling you what I intend to do. An edict will arrive any day now, requiring you to return to them with Astasiya, and it will likely also include a request to remove Sethios. Will you abide?"

Sethios didn't need to ask what that last part meant— the Seraphim would require Caro to kill him. Because that was the only way he would allow her to take his child away from him.

"I will not." Caro lifted her chin. "And if they attempt to force me, I will respond lethally. Our daughter will have a choice in her future."

"Will they even be able to find you?" Sethios asked, curious. "I mean, your skill is the ability to hide, right?"

Her eyes twinkled mischievously. "Correct, and I've been concealing myself since relocating here. The only one who can find me, other than Gabriel, is my mother, and she is lost to slumber for at least another few decades."

"The council may wake her," Leela warned. "But I'll inform you if that happens."

"You will pledge fealty too?" Caro asked, her shock evident.

"Not yet, as you'll need me on the inside and the council can't know I'm aware of this situation. That's why your brilliant son misted me here. I actually have no idea where we are on Earth right now, and since he forced me to drink from him first, our elders won't be able to track me either." She nudged Gabriel with her elbow, and he gave her a semi-irritated expression. "What? You know you're brilliant."

"Yes, but it does not require touching me."

Her eyes rolled upward. "Seriously, Gabe. You need to loosen up."

"Do not suggest it."

"Oh, I don't need to." Her expression turned positively impish as she looked him over. "You enjoyed yourself in New York City, didn't you?"

He cleared his throat. "Can we add the rune and be done here? I have some other loose ends to tie up, including taking this lust princess home."

"Lust princess?" Leela repeated with a laugh. "That's a new nickname."

He ignored her and gave Caro an imploring look. "This is the best way to protect her. Accept my proposal."

"You don't require my acceptance," Caro replied, her voice soft. "I trust you implicitly." She focused on Sethios. "It's his approval we require. Without it, I cannot grant your request."

An undeniable show of solidarity. There would be no decisions unless they were made together.

Sethios approved of her demonstration.

"Can you give us a few minutes to discuss?" He directed the request at their audience while observing Caro.

"Of course." Gabriel stepped forward with his hands in an open gesture. "May I?"

"You wish to hold her?" Sethios asked, uncertain of how he felt. He rather enjoyed having her tucked against him.

"I won't leave the house," he replied. "I just want to have a discussion with my sister regarding her future dating life."

Sethios tensed. "Dating?"

Gabriel's gaze darkened. "Yeah."

"There will be no dating." She was a baby. *His* baby. "That's just never happening." Even when she became an adult. He'd lock her away and kill all her suitors. Problem solved.

"Oh, on that we agree." Gabriel eyed Astasiya with a protective gleam in his gaze.

Leela shook her head. "She's not even two hours old, and you're both slapping her with a chastity belt."

"I have a few years to work on them," Caro murmured, her index finger brushing Astasiya's little button nose. "Don't worry." Her blue eyes grinned at Sethios. "Give her to Gabriel and let him pass on his brotherly wisdom. We'll discuss the rune and a few other things."

Sethios considered which point he wanted to argue first but caved to her request to hand Astasiya over to Gabriel. Mostly because he sensed his daughter's contentedness at going to her brother.

"How do I sense her?" he asked quietly as the two Seraphim left the room with his daughter cocooned safely in Gabriel's arms. A more pertinent thought hit him square in the chest. "Wait, can Osiris sense her? Can she be tracked? Did—"

Caro pressed a finger to his lips, her gaze alight with humor. "Our daughter is safe, Sethios. You are tied to her by blood, which is why you can feel her."

"But Osiris is my father. Can he feel her too?" Because his father's blood ran through Sethios *and* Astasiya.

Her lips pursed. "If they met, he may pick up on her familiarity without knowing why. As for finding her, he can't locate you, right? The same applies to her."

His shoulders loosened slightly, but tension still lined his limbs. "You're sure?"

"Yes. Blood bonds are most prevalent in those who commit to them, and between a parent and child. You're far more tied to Osiris then Astasiya ever will be."

He snorted. "If I could fix my connection to him, I would." Because he did not want to be linked to his father at all. About the only benefit was his gift of persuasion.

"There is…" She trailed off, her mouth twitching to the side. He raised a brow, waiting for her to finish as she battled whatever it was she wanted to say. She cleared her throat and sat up straighter while still clutching the sheet to her chest. "There's a way to fix it, but it would require a commitment."

That caught his attention. "A commitment to what?"

"Not to what, but to whom." She took a deep breath, her expression regressing to one he'd seen on her the night they met. A look of indifference. "Seraphim can form blood bonds with one another. It's rare, but it's a way of joining the lines and creating a new family of sorts. The sensations you're experiencing with Astasiya could apply to another, but it's not a temporary binding. It's... eternal."

"And it would break the link to my father."

"Essentially, yes. Because you would be establishing a new familial branch." Even her voice maintained an air of indifference, yet a slight flicker of emotion escaped through her eyes.

"Is it common for Seraphim to perform a blood bond?"

She shook her head. "No. It only happens when the Fates dictate it as necessary, and occasionally..." She drifted off, her gaze leaving his for the wall. "Seraphim seldom join unless there is a rationale for it, but I've heard of a few who bonded because they wanted to."

"For love," he translated.

Her pupils dilated. "Yes. As you can imagine, it's frowned upon, but it has happened."

"Once you form the bond, can you tie yourself to anyone else?"

Her irises lit with a fire as her attention shifted back to him. "No. That would defeat the purpose of joining in blood."

Hence why she stated it would be eternal. He studied her angelic features, so fragile in appearance but underlined with a ferocity he adored. A warrior masked under a sea of beauty. The perfect mate. The mother of his child. The woman who owned his future.

"A commitment of eternity," he whispered.

"Yes."

"That's a lot to ask."

"As is the blood bond of a Seraphim," she returned.

Fair. It wasn't just his commitment but also hers. "We would be tied together forever, angel. You sure you want that?"

"I never offered."

His lips lifted at the edges, his voice soft. "Yes, Caro. You did." Just not with words. Everything in her demeanor telegraphed her intent, especially her eyes. "Would bonding enhance my connection to Astasiya as well?"

"Yes."

"Thereby improving our ability to protect her."

Caro swallowed, her gaze returning to the wall. "Yes."

He brushed his knuckles over her cheek before sliding his palm to the back of her neck. He wanted her focus on him, not on the boring paint job in this room. "What other benefits, angel? Would you be able to pick up on my feelings and moods?"

Sadness tinged her blue irises as she met his gaze. "Yes, just as you will be able to sense mine. Our gifts would also mingle. Meaning, I should be able to persuade, perhaps even hypnotize, since you mentioned that being an ability from your mother's line. And you will be permanently hidden, as is the purpose of my bloodline."

"I see." He ran his thumb over her pulse. "What else?"

"We will be able to telegraph messages to each other, as Gabriel does to me."

"Hmm." He studied her closely. "It's quite a commitment, Caro."

Her lashes fell, sweeping her cheek as she nodded. "Yes."

"We've only known each other two months, and eternity is a long time," he added.

She nodded again, her mouth flattened into a line of tension that disabled her ability to speak.

He leaned in to brush his lips against hers. "It'll be difficult," he whispered. "And I'm certain we will have moments of regret—likely on your behalf more than mine. I'm overbearing, ruthless, and very set in my ways. And perhaps, most importantly, I am not someone a woman should choose as a faithful partner."

More nodding, agreeing with all his comments, or more likely, accepting them. Because they were truths, not opinions.

"But," he continued softly, "while I recognize my shortcomings, I also realize that with you they don't exist. You're the only one I want in my life, Caro. And I will fight for you—*for us*—throughout eternity, if you'll have me."

Three thousand years was a long time to be alive. He understood his preferences better than most, knew what he loved about life, what he hated, what he enjoyed, and what he craved. And Caro ticked every box for him.

She encouraged him to laugh. She enthralled him both inside and outside the bedroom. She fought him. She didn't fear him. She refused to yield to him.

Two months was a blink of an eye, but when one lived as long as Sethios, one learned how to read situations quickly. And Caro intrigued him in a way few ever had.

Eternity with her wouldn't be easy, but he didn't want easy. He wanted a challenge. He craved a partner who could put him in his place and excite him at the same time.

Caro embodied everything he desired and more. That their bond would enhance his ability to protect Astasiya was a significant bonus. How could he refuse such an opportunity?

"Bond with me, Caro." He cupped her cheek. "If you'll have me forever?"

Chapter Twenty-One

Blood Bonds

Caro's heart stopped beating. "You want the blood bond?"

She felt certain he would refuse, or worse, laugh at her. But as with everything Sethios did, he surprised her yet again.

He didn't hesitate. "Yes."

"Because of Astasiya?" She knew it was a very real possibility and accepted that outcome, yet she held her breath while waiting for him to respond.

"Because of you," he replied, his lips a whisper away from hers. "Because of us. This isn't short-term, Caro. It never was." His palms burned against her cheeks as he cradled her face. "We created a life together and, in the process, formed something far more powerful between us. You gifted me an experience I never knew I wanted."

Sensation thickened her throat, causing her eyes to burn. She hadn't realized how much she craved a connection with him until he agreed. It felt right, as if fate herself encouraged the union.

She swallowed, the world slowing around her. "The bond is similar to a marriage, only far more intense and eternal. Nothing can break it, not even a Seraphim as strong as you."

His lips tilted upward into a breathtaking smile. "I thought I was an abomination. Not a Seraphim."

She placed her palm over his chest. "You're Seraphim enough to me."

He might not have wings or the ability to mist, but power radiated from him like a beacon. And he drew her to him in unspeakable ways.

"You're better than a Seraphim," she clarified softly. He took care of her, taught her how to feel, introduced her to pleasure, and gifted her a beautiful daughter—one she could feel smiling through the familial bond. "You've changed me irrevocably, and I have no desire to return to my former self."

The Caro of two months ago was bored; she just didn't realize it. Now she felt more alive than ever before and had the man beside her to thank for that.

He kissed her, his tongue lightly slipping into her mouth to explore every inch in long, languid strokes. She met him move for move, her body responding to his as if living solely under his command.

"Caro," he breathed, pushing her back into the bed and settling over her. He'd exchanged his towel for jeans at some point but hadn't bothered with a shirt.

His chest burned against her bare breasts, sending delicious tingles to every nerve ending of her freshly healed form. "I'll never tire of this," she vowed, arching into him.

Sethios went to his elbows on either side of her head, the lower half of his body cradled between her thighs. "I've been with thousands of women, and men, too, when I was bored, as well as a combination of both at times. The majority of my experiences were forgettable occurrences. And honestly, nothing surprises me anymore, and my interest in new partners tends to wane quickly."

He pressed a finger to her lips when she opened them to point out that this was neither a romantic speech nor something she wanted to know. She actually preferred him to *stop* speaking.

"But," he continued, a smile in his voice, "you surprise me, Caro. At every turn. When I bargained with you that first night, I thought a few hours would satisfy my curiosity. Instead, it heightened it. And every moment since has stoked that curiosity to an eternal flame that will take centuries to dampen, perhaps even forever.

"However, it's not me who should be concerned about losing interest; it's you. I've sowed my oats thousands of times before, but you haven't. And that, my darling Caro, provides me with the biggest challenge of them all. I have to maintain your interest—for eternity."

"Something tells me your ego can handle that," she deadpanned.

He chuckled. "Oh, it's a task I'm very much looking forward to mastering. Every. Single. Day."

She tried to smile, but something still nagged at her, even as he lay atop her discussing their future intimacy. He might be right about her lack of experience being a concern for straying away from the bond, but he was the one who had admitted several times that long-term commitment wasn't his strength.

Should Sethios ever take another, Caro would require herself to do the same—if anything, to hide from the pain of his betrayal. Because that's what it would be, especially with her being able to sense his emotion through the bond.

His brow furrowed as he studied her. "I did not mean for my history to cause pain, love. I only meant to explain that my background solidifies my decision to bond with you because I've lived long enough to know being with you is a true gift of life. But you're only just experiencing pleasure and sensation for the first time; therefore, it will be on me to entertain you for eternity—physically, mentally, and emotionally."

"Are you implying that we will be monogamous?" she asked carefully.

"Yes."

She frowned. "But you just admitted a few minutes ago that a woman should not desire you for a faithful mate. Where does that leave us?"

"Forever fighting for each other," he replied. "And as I said, I'm willing to fight if you are." His mouth touched hers briefly. "I'm committed to you, our child, and us. Just say the word."

An invisible weight lifted from her chest as light danced around them. Sethios gazed at her in reverence, his irises a luminescent green. He balanced on a single elbow and traced her feathers with his opposite hand. She hadn't meant to mist.

"My angel side accepts," she whispered, her face heating. It'd been her soul that rejoiced at his words, and the burst of happiness caused her wings to flutter to life at her back. It should have hurt with the way they forced themselves between her shoulder blades and the mattress, but she was too exuberant to care.

Caro attacked his mouth with her own, putting everything she felt into their kiss and then some. He accepted and returned the favor in kind, twining his tongue with hers in a way that left her weak and shaking beneath him, and aching for more.

"One more thing to discuss, love." The words were spoken against her lips and tasted of lust and yearning. "The rune."

"If Gabriel says it will protect Astasiya, I believe him. He's spent the last several weeks investigating her future. For us."

Sethios nuzzled her nose and hummed, "Not for us, but

for her. He might hide behind a mask of stoicism, but I saw the way he looked at her."

Caro grinned because she noticed that as well. "He'll never harm her. And if I heard him right before, he's working with Ezekiel."

"Yes, he mentioned Ezekiel's plan and playing their moves right. I imagine this rune is one of them." Sethios trailed his mouth across her jawline to her neck where he nibbled the tender skin below her ear. "If you feel this is the right move, I will trust your instincts. You know more about runes than I do."

If possible, her heart grew even bigger at his words.

Trust, she realized. *A partnership.*

They would discuss these decisions among themselves and agree as a team. Always. That was the only way for this to work, and it would lay the foundation for their bond.

Perhaps she was insane to even consider tying herself to him for eternity, but it felt right. The Fates set her up to create a baby. Perhaps this was their goal all along as well, but she no longer worried about their predictions and plans. This was her life, and her decisions would be her own. Including this one.

"Then we'll give permission for the rune and allow Gabriel to pledge his fealty. It's the best way to protect her."

Sethios nodded in agreement against her neck.

"And we will perform the blood bond now," she added, feeling bold. "Bite me."

"Happily," he murmured, running his teeth against her too-hot skin. The prick of his incisors elicited a sigh from deep within, her angelic soul fluttering excitedly inside. He pulled her essence into him as her wings ruffled beneath her. She'd yet to return to her corporeal state, and perhaps she wouldn't for a bit.

Caro laced her fingers in his thick hair while he drank from her, and closed her eyes in contentment. He would need more than usual tonight, something she showed, rather than said, by holding him against her.

His body tensed above her, his muscles bunched in a way that suggested he wanted to withdraw, but she applied pressure to keep him in place and arched her neck for even greater access.

It wasn't until she felt the tingling in her toes and fingertips that she whispered, "Stop."

He pulled back, his green eyes bright with power. "That's a rush."

Yes, she imagined it would be but had never actually experienced it for herself. She laid her palm on his shoulder and nudged him off her and onto his back.

He obliged with an arched brow. "Trying to take charge, Caro?"

"I'm always in charge, Sethios," she replied, feeling tired from the loss of blood.

"You keep telling yourself that, angel."

She tried to smile, but her lips were too cold. Her wings retracted as she attempted to roll onto him. Ice slithered through her veins, weighing down her limbs.

Okay. Maybe Sethios took too much blood.

"Here." His hands caught her hips to pull her on top of him.

She pressed a grateful kiss to his chin before nuzzling his neck and finding his pulse. Yet, as she opened her mouth to bite, her jaw refused to move.

My soul isn't fully healed from the power exchange with Astasiya, she realized numbly. In her haste to bond with Sethios, she'd ignored her own angelic healing.

She tried to open her eyes to tell him that, but her throat was too raw for words. Damn. She'd have to wait until she healed again and start over.

"Angel?" Sethios lifted her chin and took in her expression. Whatever he saw made his brow furrow. "You weren't ready."

She blinked in response while her heart sighed at how well he knew her.

"Hmm." He nudged her onto her side again, cradling her

head against his shoulder, and bit the wrist of his opposite arm. Then he pressed the wound to her mouth. "Drink, love."

The first drop of his blood hit her tongue, causing her to wince. She'd never indulged in the essence of another being and didn't know what flavor to expect. He seemed to enjoy hers just fine, so she hadn't expected the bitter note.

Then it slid down her throat, and her eyes widened.

He chuckled. "Yeah, it can take a minute."

Oh.

Sweet.

So, so sweet.

Like the finest chocolate mingled with wine.

Ambrosia.

Caro swallowed another taste, her eyelids fluttering closed.

Yes. More, please.

"Take as much as you need," he whispered, his wrist pressed firmly against her lips. She licked the wound he made and created a new one with her teeth when the skin started to heal. The arm around her tensed, encouraging her to move closer to him, and she slid her calf between his jean-clad legs.

Electricity flickered between them as energy spilled from his body to hers. And, wow, did it feel amazing. She craved more of it and sucked hard, demanding more of his essence to fill her being.

"You will be doing that to my cock later," he whispered harshly.

Her thighs clenched. It would be another part of her body sucking his cock later—the part humming with the hot current flowing between them.

"Fuck," he gritted out. "I can *feel* your arousal."

She would have smiled if he hadn't hit her with a wave of his own need and desire. It shook her foundation and forced her to release his wrist on a guttural groan. She climbed onto him and took his mouth with a ferocity she felt more than understood.

"I need you. Now." Her hands moved to his jeans, unbuttoning them and forcing the zipper down to free his engorged member. She didn't give him a second to adjust or to finish removing his pants before she straddled him and put him exactly where she required him.

"Shit," he breathed, his hips bucking into hers as she rode him the way they both demanded.

Overwhelming sensations fractured her conscious, turning her into an animal of passion. Her wings appeared and disappeared at her back, her angelic side eager to play with her mate—her equal in life.

Mine.

"Yes," Sethios growled. "And mine."

God, this bond. It was far deeper than anything she'd ever felt or imagined possible. Seraphim never discussed the details, aside from the power exchange, nor had she experienced anything like this with her children or parents.

But Sethios.

Everything he did continued to amaze her, and of course, this wasn't any different.

Magic stirred around them, heightening the sensations of their joined forms and pouring static energy through her veins. She hummed with foreign and known power and quaked beneath their joined arousal.

Caro rode Sethios into oblivion, her breasts swaying with her effort and her practical senses hiding beneath a fog of sensuality.

His hands held her hips, forcing her into a vigorous rhythm that threw her into an orgasmic state. He followed her over, cascading them into a joined eternity of oblivion and pleasure. It went on for minutes, maybe hours, before she finally collapsed on top of him, exhausted.

He rolled her beneath him, his cock still fully erect inside her, and kissed her reverently. Her name whispered through the air repeatedly as he continued to move slowly and purposely within her.

"Sethios." She drew her nails down his back, arching into the ecstasy he provided. His emotions caressed her heart, displaying without words his devotion and care for her. Caro knew he desired her, but to feel the deeper adoration thriving within him, specifically for her, nearly undid her. Love was too weak of a word for such a bonding. Soul mates, maybe. Angelic partners. A new blood essence.

"A new family." The words were exhaled against her neck. "We've created something no one can break. I can feel you so deeply, Caro. All your turmoil, your worries, your pleasure, your heart." He shuddered. "Fuck, I feel everything."

"Me too," she whispered.

All his hatred for Osiris.

Sethios's fear that Caro wouldn't accept him because he was a half-breed—something he didn't even seem to realize himself.

His worry for their daughter's future.

His innate need to always protect himself first and finding for the first time in his life that he cared about not one but two beings more than himself.

She quivered beneath him as her heart grew impossibly larger. Her worries about his fidelity were for naught. He might have a past, but he only saw her in his future.

"Mine forever," he vowed.

"Forever," she agreed.

Their daughter's happiness vibrated down the line, interrupting the moment briefly but then leaving as Sethios took Caro's mouth in a carnal kiss not meant for young minds.

He claimed Caro with his tongue and body, bringing her over the edge into another cataclysmic state of bliss that splintered her world. So much sensation. So much worship. So much heart.

Nothing.

No one.

Would ever take this away from them.

A bond built to withstand time and space.

The Fates be damned. Because Sethios and Caro would survive anything and everything. Even the darkest moments blossoming on the horizon.

Part Three
Shattered Bonds

"Memento mori. Remember that you have to die."

-Osiris

Chapter Twenty-Two

The Beginning

Seven Years Later…

"Astasiya, what did I tell you about using your persuasive talent?" Sethios arched a single brow at the little blonde beside him.

She twisted her lips to the side, her green eyes thoughtful. "Not to use it on strangers," she said slowly. "But I wanted that ice cream and he wouldn't give it to me."

"That's not a reason to demand it."

She folded her arms and tried to raise her brow back at him. "But you demand Mom do things alllll the time that she doesn't want to do because *you* want somcthing."

Caro bit her lip to keep from smiling, but he felt her amusement through the bond.

Cute, he thought at her before kneeling to his daughter's level. "What I do with your mom is very different and private. Do I persuade strangers?"

Yes, Caro sent through their bond. Or he assumed that's what she was trying to say to him since he received a vision of her nodding repeatedly.

Not. Helping. He sent back to her.

Astasiya pinched her lips again and slowly shook her head. "We don't show strangers."

"And why don't we persuade strangers?" he asked, voice gentle.

"'Cause they don't understand and can make bad things happen."

Close enough. "Good girl." Having a daughter who could force people to do her bidding was not easy. Fortunately, Astasiya was far more intelligent than a typical human child. She didn't fully understand her differences but grasped enough to keep her special talents hidden.

Usually, anyway.

He stood and held out his hand for her. "Want to practice later?"

Her green eyes sparkled with excitement. "Yeah!"

Caro and Sethios tried to work with her every day on her persuasive talents. The others either didn't need fostering or weren't active yet. Thank the Fates for that because training a child how to properly use compulsion wasn't easy.

"Did he notice anything?" Caro asked as they began walking toward their car.

"Yes, but I handled it." By suggesting rather forcefully that his daughter was just adorable and hard to refuse. The older man had agreed with a bemused smile, none the wiser.

"Good. We need…" Her voice trailed off at the sight of her son leaning against their car in angelic form. His blue-and-white wings protruded proudly from his back as he observed the trio with his trademark stoicism. Except a hint of pain lurked in his gaze as he eyed his mother.

Caro glanced around the parking lot before whispering,

"Be back in a moment." She misted into her ethereal form to join her son while Astasiya glanced around in alarm.

"Gah!" His daughter stomped her foot in frustration. "Mom always cheats at hide-and-seek! She didn't even say we were playing."

He chuckled. "She's just gone off to talk to an old friend." They had collectively agreed not to introduce Astasiya to Gabriel until a later point in her life. She had enough questions about her heritage, and the Seraphim would only increase her confusion. Fortunately, she wouldn't be able to see him or any others of her kind until she grew into her own misting abilities.

"An angel friend?" Astasiya whispered loudly.

"Yes." He squeezed her hand reassuringly. "I'm sure she'll be back in…" His voice trailed off as a shock of pain traveled through the bond, hitting him directly in the chest.

"Mom!" Astasiya called out, obviously having felt it too. She tried to run toward the car, having clearly sensed where Caro had misted to, but Sethios held her back while catching his angel's gaze. Abject horror colored her expression as Gabriel disappeared.

He lifted Astasiya into his arms and walked swiftly to Caro. "What is it?"

"Seven years," she whispered, her skin pale as she took her corporeal form. "It's time."

Astasiya held out her hands for Caro, requiring her touch after sensing her mother's pain.

"I'm okay, little angel," Caro assured. "I'm okay."

"Mom hurts," Astasiya whispered. "Bad hurt."

"I know, baby. But I'm okay." She pulled their daughter into her arms and held her tight, her eyes closing. "I love you."

"I love you too, Momma," she whispered.

"I'll give you the world if I can, my precious one. Always and forever."

"I just want you, Momma."

"I know, baby. I know." Such heartbreak underlined her

voice.

Seven years.

It's time…

Sethios's stomach tightened at the resolve playing through his bond with Caro. They decided together after hearing the full prophecy of this day that they would see it through. For Astasiya.

"It's the only way," Caro whispered, repeating the words he had said when they made their choice.

Or we risk our daughter was the statement that hung between them unspoken.

"Today?" he asked.

She nodded. "That was our one-hour warning."

His heart ached as he realized this might be the last time he would see his daughter for years, perhaps even decades. There was no way to know how long it would take.

Caro handed Astasiya back to him, and he hugged her so close that she complained. But he didn't stop, his soul breaking in two as he resolved himself to this fate.

He didn't worry about himself so much as his two angels. The loves of his life.

Caro joined the hug, her aura radiating the same fierce protectiveness, except for him and their daughter.

And then she met his gaze again, her own reflecting the promise they made to one another. To overcome anything and everything in their path, regardless of how much it hurt or how challenging it became. They would never betray each other.

Mine, he told her.

Mine, she agreed.

"Let's go home," he said out loud. "We need to prepare."

Caro nodded and took the keys so he could hold Astasiya one last time on their drive. She curled into his chest, her blonde head tucked beneath his chin, and sniffled. "You're scaring me, Daddy."

"Don't be afraid, darling girl," he murmured. "You're

stronger than you know."

"Then why so sad?"

"Because sometimes life requires the ultimate sacrifice for love, and while it's the right course, it still hurts." He kissed her head and hugged her to him. "But for you, my darling little angel, I would give everything. And so would your mom. It's just time for us to prove it. That's all."

She peered up at him through damp lashes. "I don't understand."

"I know, my angel. I know." He brushed her hair from her face and pulled her back into him. "One day, I'll tell you everything. I vow it. But for today, we're going to play the ultimate game of hide-and-seek, okay? You remember that place we always go to? The one where Mommy can never find us?"

Her little brow crinkled in confusion. "Yeah?"

"When we get home, I want you to go there and not come out. No matter what happens. Understand?"

She sniffled again. "I don't wanna play today, Daddy. Please don't make me."

He smiled softly, his heart sad. "You have to play today, little angel. For me and your mom. Just in case the bad men come, okay?"

"'Cause of the ice cream?" she whispered, her eyes going wide.

Caro pulled into the driveway and shot him a look.

"No, darling, not the ice cream. The bad men who might come will be here for me and your mom, not you. So you have to stay hidden and wait for me to find you, just like all the other times we played."

Her nose scrunched. "But this time feels different."

Because you're a brilliant little girl, he thought as he opened the driver-side door. "It's the same as all the other times," he lied. "Just hide and wait for us to find you. Then we'll get some ice cream."

Caro's expression broke on his clear fabrication, but she smiled in time for Astasiya to look at her. "Go on, my darling girl. Give me a quick hug and run off to your place. Then I'll try to find you."

Sethios gave her another kiss and a hug—his version of goodbye. Then he did the hardest thing he'd ever had to do. He set her down and let her go. He knew it was the only way to protect her. Osiris had to believe Caro and Sethios were the threat to his life. They couldn't risk his father finding out about Astasiya. They had to keep her safe.

"Oh, my darling girl," Caro murmured, holding Astasiya against her chest in a tight hold. "I love you more than life itself. You know that, don't you?"

"I love you too, Momma." She kissed Caro on the cheek. "Please don't forget about me in the hiding place."

"I'll never forget about you, my little love. Never."

"Never," Sethios agreed, his throat thick with emotion. "Now go, sweet angel. Hide."

Caro stepped to his side and forced a smile for their daughter. "Go, darling. We'll find you. I vow it."

Astasiya almost seemed to question the veracity of their game and their words, but a smile and a wink from Sethios sent her running to her secret place. The one he created specifically for today.

As soon as she was out of sight, Caro collapsed against him, her body shaking with sadness. "Tell me this is the right decision," she demanded. "Tell me."

"It's the only decision," he replied softly.

"Then why does it hurt so much?"

"Because we're sacrificing our hearts," he whispered. "For love."

She shook her head against him but said no more. Because there wasn't anything left to say or do. They could only endure what was to come. For Astasiya.

He held Caro and kissed her hair, her forehead, her temple, her eyes, and her lips. Memorizing every inch of the woman he'd grown to cherish and revere throughout the years. His mate. His other half. His partner in everything.

A few decades apart wouldn't kill them.

Astasiya would save them. As long as they moved this chess piece the right way.

"Eternity," Caro whispered.

"Eternity," he agreed, kissing her soundly. Countless hours in bed and in each other's arms, and he still desired her as much as he did that first night. Perhaps even more now that they knew each other so incredibly well.

A familiar presence tickled his senses, causing him to stiffen against Caro. The only indication he could give that the hour had arrived and it was time.

"Well, it's been a long time," Ezekiel murmured, his gaze hard. He had one of the most difficult tasks of all.

"Ezekiel," Sethios returned. "This is an unpleasant surprise. To what do we owe the visit?"

A hint of pain flashed in his oldest friend's features, but he reined it in just as quickly. "Osiris would like to speak with you and the Seraphim."

"I bet." Sethios grinned. "You can tell him I refuse."

"It wasn't a request."

No, it wouldn't be one. "You had to have known we wouldn't just agree, so what do you have planned?" Sethios already knew, as did Ezekiel, but neither party could admit that without ruining the charade.

"Hmm, it's not a matter of planning, really," Ezekiel mused. "More the element of surprise."

The pistol appeared in his hand as if by magic and fired directly into Sethios's chest before he could utter a word— just the way Gabriel said it would happen. What he failed to mention was the burning sensation.

"Fu—" He couldn't finish the word as he fell to his knees, the pain excruciating. Caro screamed beside him and cut off in a gurgle as another bullet presumably hit her before she could mist.

Flames erupted from Sethios's skin, but he couldn't feel them beneath the pressure flooding his veins.

The fuck is in that gun?

"Incendiary bullets," Ezekiel explained casually.

"Jonathan's researchers developed them for the Sentinels at the CRF. I don't think the science is quite right, though, because it's not meant to be obvious. And, well, this is pretty damn obvious."

Asshole, Sethios thought at him as his body convulsed. He could feel his skin melting and mending at remarkable speeds. Being of Seraphim blood, he couldn't die. And his body worked damn hard to keep him breathing, despite whatever technology Ezekiel had shot into his system.

His blood was on fire. Literally. And if the agony traveling through the line from Caro was anything to go by, hers was too.

Shit.

That was *not* part of the plan. Neither was Ezekiel's maniacal laugh or the spike of shock traveling through the bond from Astasiya.

Through the flames engulfing him, he met a pair of terrified eyes peering at him in the distance. Fuck. She was not meant to see this. She was supposed to be hiding. *No matter what* was their promise. She'd broken it. Because of the pain echoing through the bond.

They'd failed her. Or would, anyway, if Osiris appeared now.

Run! he commanded with the remains of his energy. *Hide!*

Her expression contorted in agony as he forced her little legs to move, and then Gabriel appeared right behind her in his ethereal form. His gaze met Sethios's for a split second—just long enough to convey a reassuring nod—and the pair of them were gone.

Sethios relaxed despite his current predicament, content that his child was safe. Gabriel would guard her.

"Well," a chilling voice said above the chaos riddling Sethios's form. "I see you've finally come through, Ezekiel."

"Yes, Sire," Ezekiel replied, sounding quite pleased with himself. "I followed up on a lead that proved fortuitous."

"What lead?"

"A phone call between some shopkeeper and his wife. He claimed someone compelled him—over ice cream, of all things." Ezekiel chuckled as Sethios's heart stopped. His friend purposely left out the detail about it being a little girl who used persuasion, but if Osiris asked for clarification, this could all be for naught.

Caro must have felt the same because panic slipped through the bond even as he pushed back at her to remain calm. Already the fire engulfing them was dying, whatever chemical reaction stirred in his blood seemingly disappearing. Only five minutes at most had passed, perhaps even less time than that.

"I thought the purpose of these bullets was to disintegrate the body," Ezekiel added, cleverly distracting from the topic at hand. "I had rather looked forward to watching the Seraphim regenerate from ash."

Osiris chuckled. "Be sure to inform Jonathan that he still has work to do."

"Consider it done." Ezekiel crouched and used the pistol against Sethios's head to force his gaze upward. "Ah, there you are. Already healing, I see. Shall I shoot him again, Sire?"

"No, the toy is no longer needed. I can take it from here."

"Pity." Ezekiel stood and pocketed the gun.

"Pick up the Seraphim first. I have a few things I need from her."

Agony shot through the bond as Ezekiel followed Osiris's orders, and Sethios fought his protective instincts. It helped that he couldn't move yet, his blood still regenerating in his veins. Once the process ended, he'd have full range of his skills in hand.

"Beautiful," Osiris murmured, stepping forward. "Tell me, young one, what is your name?"

"Caro," she rasped, pain echoing from her like a beacon. The bastard had forced her to speak when her body hadn't finished rejuvenating yet.

"I'm not familiar with you." Osiris inched closer, his foot landing right beside Sethios's head. "Tell me who sent you and why."

"High Council. Edict." Her throat sounded raw, her words barely audible.

"I see." Sethios sensed more than saw Osiris scratching his chin. It was a habit of his before he wished to do something truly terrible. "Tell me the edict. Now."

Sethios flinched, his reflexes kicking in at the realization of just how cruel an order that was for someone in Caro's position. Her throat wasn't even healed yet, but she would have to say every word regardless.

"The High Council of Seraph…" She paused to cough, her voice wretched and hoarse beyond repair.

"Now, child. I don't have all day."

Sethios growled, his instincts taking over as he engaged his gift. Except when he tried to force Osiris to stop, the command fizzled into ash inside his head.

Fuck.

His father had compelled him *not* to use his gifts, which meant he'd probably also hampered Caro's ability to mist.

Still, Sethios tried again, determined. He'd never attempted to use his talent against that of his father, but their strengths didn't compare. Especially with Sethios being in a healing state.

Osiris kicked his head. Hard. "Wait your turn, Son. I'll get to you. Speak, child. Now."

The world spun as Caro obeyed. "The High Council h-hereby issues the f-following b-blood edict to Osiris."

Fuck, the words were hardly audible and sent excruciating pulses through the bond. Sethios couldn't help trying yet again to disable his father's control, but the Seraphim was too strong for him.

The only one who ever made me feel weak…

"Your i-immoral a-activities of l-late are in d-direct violation with y-your purpose on this p-plane. Using your gift for the afterlife to p-poison the blood of humanity has earned you an additional five millennia of s-solitude."

A horrendous cough sounded from her lungs, yet the edict continued to spill from her mouth under his compulsion. "L-leniency may be g-granted when, and only when, y-you rid Earth of your a-abominations. Failure to do so may yield further a-actions from the council."

She gasped, fury mingling with horror in her aura. They both knew this would hurt, but nothing could be worse than watching Osiris fuck with Astasiya in this manner.

Sethios held on to that, grasped the reminder hard, and telegraphed the resolve to Caro to bolster her energy.

"Well, that's fascinating." His father almost sounded amused. "It took you seven years to deliver that message? You must be the most incompetent messenger the High Council has ever seen. They'll thank me for taking you off their hands, I'm sure."

"I kept her," Sethios ground out, his own throat raw and sore.

"What?"

"I kept her," he repeated. "Compelled her to stay." Not a lie since that's how it all began.

"Why?"

Sethios affected the best shrug he could, given his position on the ground. "She's a good fuck." The statement hurt his heart more than his throat, especially when he felt Caro flinch beside him. "She could also mist," he added, feeling stronger by the second. "Helpful when trying to escape a madman."

"I see." A note of cruelty underlined his tone, followed by a lethal smile. "And the bond between you was forced as well?"

Sethios froze. Caro had been certain Osiris wouldn't be able to sense their connection.

What about Astasiya?

Could his father feel her as well?

Ice flooded his veins, cooling the remains of the fire that destroyed him only moments ago. He forced his head to lift, his eyes connecting with those so similar to his own.

"I demanded that as well." He put every ounce of nonchalance into his voice. "It helped hide my essence from you and Ezekiel."

"Indeed." His father tapped his chin, considering. "A logical ploy."

Sethios's shoulders relaxed infinitesimally as he gathered his strength to stand. "You know I'm all about survival."

Osiris assessed him with a flat stare. "I do, but I also know when you're lying, and on this, you are not being truthful. You love her."

Sethios chuckled even as his chest throbbed. "Do I?"

His father arched a condescending brow. "You deny it?"

He shrugged again. "I like her enough."

"And you?" Osiris shifted his focus to Caro. "Do you deny loving him?"

"Seraphim do not love." A trademark reply. Caro had even brought out her old stoic tone. The realization pleased him because it indicated she'd fully recovered from the incendiary bullet.

"But you do," Osiris murmured. "You forget I'm the Seraphim of Life. I feel your bond thriving healthily, and that requires emotional commitment." His lips twitched at the edges. "I can't wait to shatter it."

A cold chill swept down Sethios's spine. Caro said bonds were impenetrable. How could his father break it?

The note of concern flowed from Caro as well, her panic nearly overwhelming in clarity. If Osiris destroyed the connection between them, how would it impact Astasiya?

Gabriel warned that they would live in agony for an unspecified period of time but failed to mention this part. Was it something Skye hadn't predicted? Had Ezekiel betrayed them all? His gaze locked on his best friend, but his expression remained unreadable. Not even a hint of sadness floated in those ebony eyes.

Shit.

Sethios knew the assassin would do anything for Skye—

he even understood it, now that Caro had entered his life—but to hurt them in this manner? Sethios had to believe his best friend would have at least warned them.

"Ah, the silence is beautiful and proves my point. A love bond." Osiris revealed his teeth. "This will be a suitable punishment indeed and may even encourage me to allow you to live, though trust me when I say you'll both prefer death."

Neither Caro nor Sethios could speak. What was there to say? Begging would only intrigue the mad Seraphim.

"I know what you're thinking, young one," Osiris continued. "That breaking a bond is impossible, and on that, you may be correct so long as both Seraphim are alive. But when one dies, the connection falters."

"You can't kill a Seraphim," she growled. "Or, trust me, I would kill you."

"Oh, such fire!" He clapped enthusiastically. "Yes, breaking you will be such fun indeed. And, my son, I can see the allure." His gaze danced lazily over Caro in a way that caused Sethios to clench his hands into fists. "You chose well."

"Don't touch her." Sethios could handle a lot of torture, but the defiling of his mate? No. Fuck no.

What will you do about it? some dark voice whispered.

Kill him.

How?

With my bare hands.

The chuckle that responded sounded far too much like his father's, even though Sethios knew it to be impossible. Osiris did not possess telepathic abilities. It was merely Sethios's own subconscious fucking with him.

Dick.

"And there's the proof of the love match," his father mused. "I sensed it before, but now it's blossoming like the hottest of fires. How fascinating."

Sethios folded his arms. "Let me know when you're done showboating. I'm bored."

Some of the amusement fled his father's features, his emerald eyes hardening. "Bored, are you? Well, we can't have that." He scratched his chin, focus shifting to Caro. "As I said, death shatters a bond, or makes communication very difficult. And while a Seraphim will only continue to heal and be reborn, a constant state of death essentially destroys the connection."

A hint of fear traveled through the line as his words settled over them both.

"But I can't put you both out of commission; otherwise, it won't be nearly as fun." His gaze flickered to Sethios, and malicious energy poured from him. "I'll compel you to forget her and only allow you to remember when I require amusement. Meanwhile, she will be dropped into the deepest depths of the ocean, where she will remain powerless and die over and over again. For eternity."

Power rolled through Sethios as he tried futilely to break the spell his father had woven over his gifts, while the monster before them merely smiled.

Caro grabbed Sethios's hand, squeezing hard. A vision of their vows to one another flashed inside his thoughts, a reminder of what they promised.

Sometimes love requires the ultimate sacrifice, she was telling him. *We will find each other again. Eternity.*

Her acceptance of their fate both enraged and enthralled him. While he would do anything he could to protect their child—a being Osiris was clearly unaware of—to give up his memories of his time with Caro and allow her to be buried beneath the waves...

Fuck.

He refused.

But he was helpless to stop it. His talents, as strong as they were, barely rose inside of him. Because Osiris had snuffed out his inner flame.

"I really expected more of a fight," his father murmured. "Pity to see you've yet to tap into your full potential after all these centuries."

"Why do I think you have something to do with that?"

"Because you're my son," Osiris replied, his lips curled. "And you know me better than most. Now. Shall we get on with it?"

Sethios opened his mouth to say something sarcastic, but in the blink of an eye, he couldn't remember what the retort he had lined up was or why he even had one to say.

Odd.

He glanced around, confused by their surroundings.

Montana.

Right. He owned property here. An escape when he wanted to hide. Must have been one hell of a night.

A warm palm against his hand had him looking down and then up at the most beautiful creature he'd ever laid eyes on.

Ah, he'd spent the night entertaining this beauty. Pity he couldn't remember their time together. It must have been painful, if the glint of hurt in her gaze was anything to go by.

Hmm. Why did that suddenly elicit a deep sadness inside his chest?

She stared at him with such torment that he actually felt it. How bizarre. He wiped the tear away from her cheek and smiled. "It's all right, gorgeous. I promise to be nicer next time."

Her lashes fell as her shoulders hunched with inscrutable suffering. What had he done to her last night? She appeared unscathed enough. Perhaps the marks were hidden by her clothes. He did enjoy hiding his love bites between a woman's thighs.

Another pang sliced him wide open, confusing all his senses.

What the fuck is happening to me?

"I hate you," she whispered. "I will kill you one day." The vehemence in her voice shocked him, but not nearly as much as the reply that followed.

"No, young one. You won't."

Sethios met the gaze of his father. "What are you doing here, Dad?"

"Solving a problem," he answered easily. "Return to the estate with Ezekiel while I handle your garbage."

Sethios let go of the woman's hand with a shrug. It's not like she'd been all that remarkable. "Of course. Enjoy."

Another pang slammed into his abdomen, causing him to flinch. Then he met the gaze of the angel beside him and blinked. For just a moment, he could swear he knew her. Then the sensation disappeared as quickly as it arose.

Strange.

He clearly needed a shower and perhaps a heavy drink.

Ezekiel stood waiting, hand outstretched, gaze shadowed.

Sethios frowned. *What are you hiding, old friend?*

His brain fought to solve the puzzle around him—how he ended up there, why he felt such a real connection to the strange woman beside him, why his father was here in what Sethios considered to be his favorite safe haven…

I've never told Osiris about this place. Or Ezekiel. Sethios planned to use it as a retreat should he need it.

His gaze caught and held the beautiful blue eyes of the blonde. Then a vision of him holding her flashed through his mind. Another vision of their lovemaking. A small blonde girl. Their daughter? A life he knew nothing about. Nor one he would ever have desired.

"You're a Seraphim," he realized, looking her over. "A bewitching one at that."

"Don't worry about her," his father said. "I'll handle everything. Just go with Ezekiel and wait for me."

The hint of persuasion in his tone forced Sethios to take a step forward. He rolled his eyes. "I'm already going, Father. No need for the theatrics."

"You know how I enjoy a good show."

Unfortunately, Sethios did. With a final glance at the too-familiar woman, he held out his hand for Ezekiel and watched her vanish from view.

His heart vibrated with agony, causing him to lose his breath as the familiar walls of his old room appeared around him. He fell to his knees with a cry, his world unhinged.

"What's happened?" he demanded, his voice hoarse.

"Welcome to my world" was all Ezekiel said as he stepped away.

Sethios stared after him, his body too weak to move.

His pulse raced with a sudden fear centering in his gut and radiating through his veins. It left him winded and pained, but he didn't know the cause. Yet the face of the gorgeous Seraphim filtered through his mind, her emotions a live current inside of him.

He rocked as her terror sifted through his being, followed by a stinging to his lungs.

Fuck. He couldn't breathe.

Water infiltrated every pore, causing him to gurgle on air.

It felt as if his room had been submerged at the bottom of the sea, yet he could see the sunlight streaming through his open windows.

None of it made sense.

But it fucking hurt. His entire body vibrated with it, shaking with the need to inhale and burning when salt penetrated his insides.

I'm dying, he realized.

Drowning.

In his own room.

He curled into a ball as tears streamed down his face because it wasn't the agony of life slipping through his fingertips that hurt most, but the sense of loss that filled him. A connection breaking that he cherished so deeply yet knew nothing about.

As the last vestiges of his consciousness melted away, a foreign name drifted through his thoughts. One that would forever live inside his heart.

Caro…

EPILOGUE

Gabriel flinched as the bond with his mother broke yet again.

He'd hoped to use their connection to find her, to release her from her prison, but Osiris dropped her in the ocean somewhere, and Gabriel had no chance of determining her location alone. It would require a far more powerful being, that of the young girl holding his hand.

After a week of gaining her trust and reaffirming their bond through the fealty he'd pledged to her as an infant, she'd finally stopped crying. Watching her parents' bodies go up in flames had not been part of the plan, but her curious mind and strong heart had pulled her from the hiding place and toward her parents' agony. Had Gabriel not shown up when he did, the results could have been catastrophic.

Alas, he had her safe and sound in Havre, Montana.

The home was one of his choosing, a family who knew everything about him and the special girl he was about to leave in their care.

No one else knew, not even Caro and Sethios. He couldn't risk Osiris breaking them and obtaining the location of their daughter. As far as everyone else knew—including Ezekiel for now—Gabriel would be the one to raise her, but his part would come into play later.

"Ready?" he asked softly.

She shook her head, her little body shaking.

"They'll protect you, just like your parents did."

She bit her lip and eyed the home. "But Momma keeps talking to me. She needs help."

He grimaced in understanding. His mother, despite likely trying not to telegraph, kept sending agonizing images of her repeated deaths through the bond. It would dwindle as time went on, hopefully only pestering Astasiya in her dreams. If not, he would alter the rune on her back enough to help give her a semblance of peace.

"I'll search for your mom," he vowed. "While you live here, okay? And then one day, we'll go find her together."

"Promise?" she asked, those green eyes holding his with an intensity unusual for a seven-year-old.

"I vow it," he replied, squeezing her hand. "We'll find her."

"Together," she demanded.

"Together," he agreed. *When you're ready.*

"Gabriel," a soft voice whispered. The hint of navy wings touched his vision as the Seraphim he recruited for this necessary task appeared beside him.

Time to say goodbye, he thought.

His heart gave an odd little pang for the tiny blonde child holding his hand. He refused to analyze it and dropped to one knee before her. Such intelligence and power lurked in her gaze, but she deserved to have a childhood. And he was determined to give her one.

"Astasiya," he murmured. "You won't remember me when we meet again, but I will make sure you know the truth when the time is right."

Her tiny brow puckered with a frown. "But I know you."

"Yes, but to keep you safe, I need you to forget me. For now." He met Vera's patient stare. "Everything from this week, including Osiris if she saw him."

"What about the death?" she asked.

"She needs that to grow," he replied. "And Ezekiel needs to be the villain."

Vera nodded. "I can do that. Anything else?"

"Yes. Give her doubts about Caro's true nature."

"That's going to be difficult."

"Indeed, that's why I called the best memory manipulator in existence for assistance." He shifted his focus to the very confused child beside him. "Consider me your personal Seraphim, Astasiya. I'll always be looking over you." He kissed her on the forehead—much to the shock of the Seraphim observing the exchange—and stood. "Now, Vera."

"Already started," she whispered.

He nodded. "Goodbye, little sister." Gabriel faded as he watched, his finger grazing the doorbell before disappearing completely.

The Davenports would raise her now, with several guardian angels standing silently beside them.

We will meet again. Soon.

The Story Will Continue with *Angel Bonds*

IMMORTAL CURSE SERIES
What's Next

Dear Reader,

Thank you for reading *Blood Bonds*. I never expected to share this story. Caro and Sethios have always been in my head, their history something I knew because it shaped the world, but I felt compelled to finally write it. And I'm very glad I did.

Stas and Issac are up next in *Angel Bonds,* which takes place 18 years after the events in the epilogue of *Blood Bonds*. Will Stas finally discover the truth about her origins? Or will she realize her potential too late?

Lastly, because I know you're all wondering: What about Sethios and Caro? Let's just say, I'm nowhere near done with them yet. ;-)

For sneak peeks, book discussions, and other fun reveals, please join my reader group on Facebook, or sign up for my newsletter. I really appreciate you taking the time to learn more about Caro and Sethios. I hope you enjoyed them as much as I did. <3

Cheers xx
Lexi

Blood Bonds
Music Playlist

"We Gotta Get Out of This Place" – Denmark + Winter
"World of Shame" – Ego Likeness
"Rescue Me" – Eurielle
"You Said" – Eurielle
"Lithium" – Evanescence
"Remember Everything" – Five Finger Death Punch
"Heavy In Your Arms" – Florence + The Machine
"Hurts Like Hell" – Fleurie
"Haunting" - Halsey
"Immortalized" – Hidden Citizens
"Heaven's a Lie" – Lacuna Coil
"Where Do We Go From Here?" – Ruelle
"Wicked Game" – Theory of a Deadman

ACKNOWLEDGMENTS

Wow. This book was probably one of the most emotional stories I've had the pleasure of writing. It took a lot of special people to help make it perfect.

First, as always, Matt: I could not do this without your support. I know I say this all the time, but thank you for putting up with me and the insanity in my head. I love you.

Allison: Thank you for reading and rereading, and reading again, and all the late-night conversations. I would be lost without you as my alpha reader!

Tracey: Thank you for being my brave beta reader who didn't mind having all of *Angel Bonds* essentially spoiled in advance. Also, thank you for understanding that Sethios is mine, and making sure the world knows it. ;-)

Casey: Thank you for providing developmental edits. I know I didn't agree with everything, which is probably Sethios's fault, but I really appreciate all your feedback and advice! One day, we will do a series bible. One day…

Louise & Melissa: Gah, my "minions." I love you both so much! Especially all the photos, comments, support, and laughs.

Bethany: You are my rock. Seriously. All the hard work and effort you put into editing my work is so very much appreciated. Thank you for always answering my questions and forgiving my misunderstanding of proper punctuation (#CommasAreEvil).

Barb, Delphine & Pam: You all are so amazing. You catch all the proofing errors, provide content feedback, and keep me honest where I need it most. I heart all three of you. <3

Julie: THANK YOU FOR SAVING MY COVER! Yes. All caps. It's deserved. You are my savior. The wings… Gah. I love them!

Famous Owls: Y'all keep me alive. Thank you for your support, social media tags, shares, comments, love, and friendship.

And to the readers: Thank you for reading Caro and Sethios's story. Their story touched me in a way I can't explain. I shouldn't have favorites, but… ☺

Thank you all! <3

ABOUT THE AUTHOR

USA Today Bestselling Author Lexi C. Foss is a writer lost in the IT world. She lives in Atlanta, Georgia with her husband and their furry children. When not writing, she's busy crossing items off her travel bucket list. Many of the places she's visited can be seen in her writing, including the mythical world of Hydria which is based on Hydra in the Greek islands. She's quirky, consumes way too much coffee, and loves to swim. Cheers!

ALSO BY LEXI C. FOSS

Immortal Curse Series
Blood Laws
Forbidden Bonds
Blood Heart
Elder Bonds
Blood Bonds
Angel Bonds

Blood Alliance Series
Chastely Bitten
Royally Bitten

Dark Provenance Series
Daughter of Death
Divinity of Acheron
Paramour of Sin

Mershano Empire Series
The Prince's Game
The Charmer's Gambit
The Rebel's Redemption
The Devil's Denial